Man in the Shadows

OTHER CLIFF HARDY THRILLERS

Man in the Shadows

A short novel and six stories

Peter Corris

Sydney
UNWIN PAPERBACKS
Wellington London

First published in Australia
by Unwin Paperbacks 1988

UNWIN PAPERBACKS
Allen & Unwin Australia Pty Ltd
An Unwin Hyman company
8 Napier Street, North Sydney NSW 2059 Australia

Allen & Unwin New Zealand Limited
60 Cambridge Terrace, Wellington, New Zealand

UNWIN PAPERBACKS
15-17 Broadwick Street, London W1V 1FP England

© Peter Corris 1988

National Library of Australia
Cataloguing-in-Publication entry:

Corris, Peter, 1942- .
    Man in the shadows.

    ISBN 0 04 320226 8.

    I. Title.

A823'.3

The characters and events in this book are fictitious,
and any resemblance to actual persons or events is
purely coincidental.

Set in 10/11pt Century Schoolbook by
Graphicraft Typesetters Limited, Hong Kong
Printed in Australia by The Book Printer,
Maryborough, Victoria.

Contents

For
PATRICK GALLAGHER

Man in the Shadows

1

A long shadow fell across the corridor outside my office. The shadow obscured the scuffed lino tiles on the floor and almost touched the card thumbtacked to the door. The card reads 'Cliff Hardy—Investigations'. It's not the original card, not the one I pinned up almost fifteen years ago, but it's very like it. I've always felt that a nameplate or stencilled letters might bring bad luck, so I've stuck with the card.

I walked towards the door and a man stepped from the shadow. He was tall and thin and I instantly felt that there was something wrong with him. Not something to make me reach for a gun, if I'd been wearing one, but something to be sorry for. It was there in the way he moved—slowly and tentatively—and in the way he stood as I came closer. He looked as if he might suddenly flinch away, retreat and dive down the fire stairs.

'Mr Cliff Hardy?' he said. He swung the small zippered bag he was carrying awkwardly.

'That's right.'

'You . . . investigate things?'

I pointed to the card. 'That's what it says. You want to come inside?'

The question seemed to cause a struggle within him. He wasn't a bad looking man—under thirty, full head of dark hair, good teeth, regular features, but there was something missing. His face was immobile and was like a painting which the artist hadn't quite finished off. But he nodded and moved closer as I unlocked the door.

'Thank you,' he said.

I got him settled in the client's chair. He put his bag on the floor beside him. For some reason that I couldn't account for, I pulled my chair out from behind my desk and sat more or less across from him with nothing in between. He wore a grey suit, white shirt, no tie. I smiled at him. 'I usually start by asking my client for a name. I don't always get the real one.'

'Gareth Greenway,' he blurted.

'Okay, Mr Greenway, how can I help you?'

He looked slowly around the room. There wasn't much to see—filing cabinet, desk, calendar on one wall, a bookcase of paperbacks and a poster from a Frida Kahlo exhibition. 'You haven't got any recording devices or anything like that, have you, Mr Hardy?'

'No, nothing like that.'

'Good. Have you ever heard of psychosurgery?'

'Yes.'

'Psychosurgery was performed on me nine months ago against my will.'

I let out a slow breath as I studied him more closely. There were no physical signs; he didn't twitch or dribble, but he had the air of an alien, of someone for whom everything around him was strange and new. 'How did that happen, Mr Greenway?'

'I don't know. That's the problem. I can't remember. I know I was in the hospital for some time.'

'What hospital?'

'Southwood Private Hospital. It's what you'd call a loony bin.'

That was the first flicker of aggression I'd seen; he opened his eyes wider as he spoke and seemed to be flinching back, although in reality he didn't move a muscle. I didn't react; I'd seen enough psychoanalytical movies to know how to behave. 'Go on,' I said.

'They did this to me, made me like this, and I don't know why. All I know is that they're going to do it to Guy and they've got to be stopped.'

'Who's Guy?'

'He was my friend, my only friend, in there.'

'I see. Why do you think he'll be ... treated the way you were?'

'This is the hard part,' he said. 'I don't know why. I just have these impressions. They won't come together properly. That's what things are like since they cut into me. That's the idea. You don't make connections between all the things that're wrong in your life so they don't bother you as much. You see?'

'Yeah.'

'Well, it didn't quite work with me. I'm still bothered. They tell me I was violent. I don't feel violent anymore. I was an actor. I couldn't act now, I wouldn't know how. That's what it does to you. How would you like it, Mr Hardy? Would you trade in all your anxieties for the sort of peace of mind that stopped you from doing what you do now? Even if that's what causes the anxieties? I assume you have some?'

'Sure,' I said. 'No, I wouldn't. What do you mean about it being the hard part?'

He leaned forward. 'I've been to see the police, doctors, the health authorities, everyone. They won't listen. I know, from something I saw or heard that I can't ... reassemble now, that Guy is in danger and that that place is hell on earth. But no one will listen because I've been certified insane and psychosurgeried. I'm a vegetable, I've got no rights, I ... '

'Easy. Why did you come to me, Mr Greenway?'

'Annie Parker told me to.'

'Annie Parker!' That made me sit back and set memories running. Annie was a heroin addict I'd had some dealings with a few years back. The daughter of an old friend, she'd been in big trouble which I'd extricated her from. She'd gone to England. 'Is Annie at this hospital?'

'She was. She died of an overdose a while back. We used to talk. Annie was pretty wrecked; some money she'd inherited from her mother was keeping her going.'

'I see.'

'You probably don't. I've got a few thousand dollars. I can pay you.'

'To do what?'

'To help me get Guy out of there. To stop him ending up like me. To save his life.'

He put his back against the chair rest and held himself straight. He looked tired suddenly, almost exhausted by the effort he'd made. I felt confused. I was sympathetic towards him; he seemed like a serious, responsible person who'd taken a terrible knock. He had a friend he cared about. I'd cared about Annie and her mother. It should have been straightforward, but mental illness and the medical profession set up strong feelings.

He waited for me and I floundered.

Do you want to be on the side of the patients or the doctors? I thought. Neither. Don't touch it. Walk away. Say you're sorry and go out and have a drink in memory of Annie and all the other damaged people you've helped but not enough to make any difference.

'Tell me more,' I said.

2

GREENWAY gave me five hundred dollars in cash which was unusual but not something for me to tear my hair out over. Then he surprised me by standing up, grabbing his bag and jerking his head at the door. 'You've got a car, haven't you?'

'Sure.'

'I don't like small rooms very much. Let me show you the place we're talking about.'

We went down to the lane at the back of the building where I keep my 1984 Falcon on a slab of concrete Primo Tomasetti the tattooist rents to me. Primo was standing in the lane having a smoke. He recently declared his tattoo parlour a No Smoking zone on a trial basis. He looked at the car which has replaced a 1965 model, same colour, fewer miles, less rust.

'Looks great, Cliff,' he said. 'Just like you'd be with a facelift.'

'Are you thinking of going into that business?' I asked him. 'It's only a sort of sideways move.'

'Yeah,' he said. 'The first'd be the toughest. You volunteering?'

Greenway was standing by, not paying any attention. I unlocked the passenger door and opened it for him. He got in slowly and gracefully. Primo stared. 'Who is he?' he whispered. 'A doctor?'

I winked at him. 'The Pope's grandson. Keep it under your hat.'

It was the last week in March. Daylight saving was a recent memory and the sun was still high in the late afternoon and a problem as I was driving into it. I asked Greenway to get my sunglasses out of the glove box.

'You should have better ones than these,' he said. 'These are shit.'

'I lose 'em; leave 'em places. Makes no sense to buy good ones. Aren't you hot? Take your jacket off.'

I was in shirt sleeves, light cotton trousers and Chinese kung fu shoes; behind the windscreen it was like a greenhouse as we drove into the sun. I was sweating freely.

'I don't feel the heat or the cold. Not since the treatment.' I glanced at him; sweat was running down the side of his face and wilting his shirt collar.

'Tell me about this place. I thought they were under strict supervision. Aren't there . . . visitors, or something? Official inspections?'

He snorted. 'The visitors are senile hacks. *They* should be in there, not . . . the patients . . . us. You'll see. The place? It's like a concentration camp. Fences, out of bounds areas. Cells . . . '

'Cells? Come on.'

'You'll see.'

'How? If it's a registered private hospital we can't just walk in and make a private inspection.'

'I know a way in. Don't worry.'

I was worried, very worried. For the rest of the drive I watched Greenway closely. He appeared to take no interest in the surroundings, spoke briefly to give me directions, and otherwise seemed to be asleep with his eyes open. We were forced to a crawl by the road works at Tom Uglys bridge where they're putting in another span. I followed the signs to Sutherland.

'You know Burraneer Bay?' Greenway said abruptly.

'Heard of it.'

'That's where we're going. Left here.'

I followed the road through Gymea into the heart of the peninsula. The houses tended to be big on large blocks with expensively maintained lawns and carefully placed trees; a few were smaller and struggling to keep up appearances. Greenway directed me past the bowling club towards the water where the houses seemed to be craning up for a good view. We stopped in a short cul-de-sac occupied by a few Spanish-style houses; one had added a mock Tudor effect for insurance. The street ended in thick bush.

'Turn the car around,' he said.

Five hundred dollars made him the boss for three days. I turned the car so it was facing back up the street. Greenway got out carrying his bag. For the first time I wondered what was in it.

'Have you got a gun?' he said.

'No.'

'Good. The hospital's down here.' He pointed to the trees. 'We can take a look from the high ground and I know where we can get through the fence.'

'Why?'

He looked at his watch. 'It's exercise time. I want to see that Guy's all right. That's all. We can talk about what to do next afterwards.'

He was suddenly much more decisive and alert. I was still worried; I wanted time to think about it but he plunged into the bush ahead of me and I followed him, feeling confused but protective. The trees shut out the light and made it seem later in the day than it was. I squinted ahead as Greenway forged on, pushing branches aside and crunching dried leaves underfoot. Then we were through and light flooded over a large open space ringed around by a high cyclone fence. There were buildings inside the area, concrete paths, garden beds. I saw a swimming pool and a tennis court half buried in shadow.

The blue water of Port Hacking hemmed in all the land. The sun still lit up the western edge but the advancing shadows were turning the water darker by the second.

Greenway tugged at my arm. 'Down here.'

We scrambled along the perimeter until he located a section of fence where the metal post was standing slightly askew. He hooked his bag over one shoulder, gripped the post and heaved. It came out of the ground; the fence sagged close to the ground for five metres on either side. Greenway trampled over it. 'Come on!' he shouted.

He raced down the slope towards the centre of the compound. I could see light shapes moving slowly around behind a hedge. What could I do? Stand there and watch? I ran after him, more with the idea of hauling him back than going with him, but he was covering the ground like Darren Clarke.

I lost breath yelling something but I couldn't have caught him anyway. He made it to the hedge as I was still skeetering down the slope. He opened his bag, pulled out a camera and started taking flash pictures. The sudden, flaring lights panicked the people behind the hedge. I heard screams and curses. Greenway raced along, stopping and shooting. I pounded after him. Three men came from behind the hedge; Greenway ducked back and they reached me first.

'It's all right,' I gasped. 'Don't . . . '

Two of them came at me; I balked and made them collide. One recovered and threw a punch which I side-stepped. I pushed him back.

'Hardy!' Greenway's yell was desperate, panicked. The third man was rushing him, reaching for the camera. Instinctively, I lunged forward and tripped him. Greenway dodged and headed back up the hill, feet digging in, well-balanced and surging.

'Hey!' I yelled. I lost balance on the uneven ground.

The man I'd pushed loomed over me; he chopped down on my neck in a perfect rabbit punch. I felt it all along my spine and down to my legs. I flopped flat, as breath and vision and everything else left me.

3

THE sun was shining in my eyes and it was only a couple of metres away. I twisted my head and that hurt more than the burning sun. I tried to lift my arm to block out the light; my shoulder was stiff and painful but I got my hand across my face.

'He's all right,' a voice said.

'Who's all right?' I said.

'You are.' This was another voice. 'Do you know where you are?'

'Hospital grounds.'

'You're inside the hospital. You've been unconscious.'

I tried to lift the upper part of my body from what I discovered was a narrow bed. It hurt and someone tried to hold me down but I got there. Everything swum around—room, faces, my legs stetched out in front of me for all of two metres. I closed my eyes. That was better. My neck hurt probably worse than my shoulder. Nothing else hurt very much. My mouth was dry.

'Some water, please.'

I opened my eyes when I felt the glass held to my mouth, took a sip and swallowed. Much better.

'A possible concussion?' one of the voices said. A shadow fell across me. 'I'm Dr Grey. Just lie back and let me examine you.'

I did it. Why not? As awakenings from physical attacks go it was much better than most. I felt strong hands on my temples; the light shone again but this time the sun had gone back up where it belonged.

'Look left, look right, look up. Possible concussion, but I think not.'

I could feel sympathy and concern waning so I stayed lying down. The next voice was milder. 'I'm Dr Smith. I want your explanation for what happened.'

I looked at them through half-opened eyes. Grey was a bulky man with heavy spectacles. He wore a white skull cap like a surgeon which was an alarming thing to see from my position. 'I was trying to be non-violent, Doctor. I pushed one man and tripped another. Then someone clobbered me.'

'That is not funny.' Grey said. 'You trespassed in the company of another man who behaved in a way calculated to disturb some already very disturbed people. You . . . '

'Where is he? Did he get away?'

'Listen to me! You are in serious trouble.'

I sat up again and took the water from the man I took to be Dr Smith. He was an older, gentler-looking type wearing similar clothes to Grey—white coat over shirt and tie. Another man stood by the door in the white-painted, almost chilly room. He was the rabbit puncher. 'I'm a little confused, Doctor,' I said. 'I may owe you an apology. Things sort of got out of control.'

'That's not good enough,' Grey spluttered. 'I want . . . '

'Now, Bruce,' Smith said, 'I think we have a reasonable man here. I'm the administrator of the hospital, Mr Hardy. We should be able to straighten things out.'

Grey didn't like that. 'I've got a half dozen people down there who're going to need special treatment for days over this, maybe longer. This bloody hooligan . . . '

Even though I wasn't at my most acute I could tell that Grey was under more pressure than was good for him. He was red in the face and a purple vein was throbbing under the flushed skin near his right eye. 'Have you called the police?' I asked.

'No.' Grey bit down hard on the word.

I drank some water and handed the glass back to Smith. 'Perhaps you should.'

'I don't think that's necessary,' Smith said. 'Just tell us what you and the other man were doing.'

'You have to see it from my point of view, Doctor. I'm here in some part of a building I'm not familiar with in the company of three men who could be axe murderers for all I know.' I pointed to the man at the door. 'I know he delivers a good hit. You know my name so I assume you've taken my wallet. I just don't feel safe.'

'This is absurd,' Grey snorted.

'So, call the police. What's stopping you?' I swung my legs off the bed and put my feet gingerly on the floor. I wondered if I could support my weight. A pratfall wouldn't have created the right impression just then.

'What circumstances would make you feel more comfortable, Mr Hardy?' Smith said.

Any public place, I thought. Preferably where they serve drinks. 'What about your office? With a view of the gate, a few people around, a telephone on the desk and my wallet in my hand.' I pointed again. 'I can do without him and I wouldn't mind a drink.'

Smith smiled. 'Happily, my office has a view of the gate and of the water and I've got a good single malt. How does that sound?'

We sat in Smith's pleasant office, admired the view and I rubbed the back of my neck. I examined my wallet and put it in my pocket.

'Now,' Smith said, 'try this.' He poured the

whisky; I sipped it and nodded. Smith took a sip and favoured me with one of his benign smiles. 'What were you up to?'

That made it sound almost like a schoolboy prank. I could've climbed through the window and walked to the front gate. There were no men bigger than me around, no guns. I wondered why I still had a sense of extreme danger.

'I was hired by a man who had undergone psychosurgery here. He said he had a friend named Guy who was in danger of receiving the same treatment. He was very upset about it. I got the impression he wanted my help in securing Guy's release.'

'I see.' Smith drank some more whisky. He swung around to a table on which there was a fair sized computer with a monitor to match. His back was turned to me as he took something from his pocket. I recognised it as my notebook. The neck punch must have fogged me because I hadn't realised it was missing. Smith flicked open a page, nodded and closed the book. He tapped keys for a while, consulted the screen and tapped some more. I finished my drink and looked at the view.

Smith swivelled slowly away from the screen until we were face to face; he handed me the notebook and reached for the bottle. I shook my head. 'Moderation,' he said. 'An excellent thing. We have a mystery on our hands, Mr Hardy. This hospital has never had a patient of the name your client gave you, that is, Gareth Greenway, and does not have one with the name of Guy—either as a first or second name.'

4

I accepted the second drink and began to wonder whether it might not be better to feel slightly drunk rather than very foolish. The shadows from the trees had spread across the surface of the water so that it was uniformly dark. The trees were moving in the light breeze but the water was still. A nice view, but it gave me no ideas.

'I assume you have an address for your Mr Greenway?' Smith said. 'Some ... documentation other than your notes?'

'No. He paid me in cash and we came straight from my office to here. I suppose I thought I'd attend to the formalities later.'

'That sounds rather unprofessional.'

I let it ride and took another sip of the good, smooth whisky, the stuff that soothes away words like 'unprofessional'. My mind jumped to the newspaper item I'd read about the course in 'Private Agency Practice' that was going to be a prerequisite for people in my business henceforth. I had a feeling I'd just failed Elementary Precautions I.

'This puts you in a rather difficult position, Mr Hardy. You could be charged with trespass, assault and so on.'

I grunted.

'But it seems more important to know what Greenway, or whoever he is in reality, was doing. You agree?'

'I'd certainly like to have a private talk with him.'

'Precisely. So would I. Would you consider a commission from me to locate him and throw some light on this unfortunate affair?'

I finished the second drink and was sure I didn't want any more. I could smell 'deal' or possibly 'fix' and you need a clear head when those things are in the air—whether you intend to accept or not. 'I'm not sure of the ethics of that,' I said.

'Surely in your business ethics have to be flexible.'

'Like in yours. Do you do psychosurgery here?'

'Yes. I could introduce you to some people who're very grateful for the fact.'

'No thanks.'

'You are ignorant and prejudiced.' There was some steel in Smith under the blandness. I stood up and fought the giddiness that swept over me. When I was steady I slapped my pockets. 'Where're my car keys?'

'I've no idea. You can leave by the front gate, Mr Hardy, but let me say this to you.' Smith walked past me; his sure, firm movements seemed to emphasise my own rockiness. He pulled open the door. 'I'll put it no firmer than this—you have committed offences that could bring your licence to practise into question. I'm quite well connected in legal and public service circles and I can be a vindictive man.'

'Maybe you should have that quality cut out of you.' I went through the door.

'I will expect to hear something from you about your supposed client within a few days, Mr Hardy. Or you will be hearing things you will not like. I can assure you of that.'

'Thanks for the drink,' I said, but I said it to a closed door. I went down a short passage past a receptionist's booth where a woman in a starched white uniform smiled at me with starched white teeth. I went out the door and down a short path to

15

a gate in the high fence. The double gates, wide enough to admit a truck, were locked and so was the smaller single gate. I looked back at the building and caught a flash of teeth. A buzzer sounded and the gate jumped open.

It took me half an hour to locate my car and quite a few minutes to get a successful hotwire start; on the old Falcon I could do it in seconds. I hadn't eaten lunch and since then I'd absorbed a good rabbit punch, two large whiskies and some humiliation. I drove home slowly, parked down the street and on the other side in a spot where I could look the house over. If anyone had visited with my keys during my absence they'd been careful. The gate that doesn't quite close was in the not-quite-closed position as before; the local newspapers looked to be arranged in the same way they had been in the morning when I stepped over them.

Inside I sniffed the air for an unfamiliar smell but it was all too familiar—the rising damp, the cat's piss on the carpet and the scent of frangipani that drifts in through the louvre windows at the back of the house. I checked the answering machine in case 'Gareth Greenway' had phoned with an explanation and apology. No such luck. The phone rang and I snatched it up.

'Mr Hardy? This is Dr Smith. I'm glad to see you got home all right. It occurred to me that you were in no condition to drive.'

'I'm tough, but I'm touched by your concern. Also I'm lucky.'

'Yes, you are. We've found your keys. You can pick them up the next time you're here.'

'You seem pretty sure I will be.'

'Yes. Any kind of negative publicity is bad for a hospital. If this Greenway is some kind of ratbag journalist . . . '

'You've got a problem. Okay, Dr Smith, I'm sure we'll be talking again.'

16

I hung up and sat down to worry. That did no good. I ate a tuna sandwich to tone up my brain cells, took some aspirin for the pain and some more whisky for the humiliation and went to bed.

Aspirin and whisky don't make for very good sleep. I woke up a couple of times, once because the cat was yowling outside. I got up and played it a tune on the can opener. Later a backfire on Glebe Point Road woke me and left me staring at the ceiling for an hour.

It was the frangipani that got me to thinking about Helen. She'd given it to me in its big tub as a gift, transported it all the way from her Bondi flat balcony, when she'd finally made the decision to go back to her husband and her kid on a full-time basis. Our six-monthly polygamous set-up hadn't worked. 'It never does,' people drunk and sober had told me. They were right.

I got up and made a cup of weak coffee and sat thinking about how I'd dragged Helen down from Kempsey to Sydney. How we'd pledged this and that and fucked until we ached. Then we'd talked until our mouths were dry and all the words were changing their meanings.

I put the coffee down and it went cold. I wanted to smoke but there was nothing available. Helen had smoked one Gitane a day which left no packets, not even any butts, lying around. As a little light seeped into the bedroom I remembered the last scene, played out right here. The tears and goodbyes. And the bloody frangipani. I could still smell it as I finally fell asleep.

5

I came awake fast and nervous. The hammering sounded as if it was on my bedroom door. Then I realised that it was downstairs. I grabbed a dressing gown, almost tripped on the stairs and reached the door in a foul temper. The knocking kept on. I jerked the door open.

'What in hell's . . . ?'

'Let me in, quick!'

'Who're you?'

'Annie Parker. Quick!' The person who was supposed to be dead slipped past me into the hall.

'Have you got a gun? Jesus, they'll be here any minute.'

'Who?' I'd asked three questions in a row and was getting sick of it.

She moved down the hall. 'Please. You know me. Annie. Just get the gun and stand in the door and let them see it. Please!'

The way she flattened herself against the wall like a back lane fighter convinced me. I got the .38 from the cupboard under the stairs, checked that the safety was on and stood in the doorway with the gun held low but in view. I felt ridiculous; dressing gown, bare legs and cold feet. A red Mazda stopped outside the house. It edged back a little so that the driver could get a better look at me. All I saw was a pale face and a turned up collar. I couldn't see his passenger at all. The car engine purred for about half a minute, then the driver revved it and moved off fast.

I closed the door and looked at the woman sitting on the bottom stair. She was medium-sized with light hair; she had on heavy sunglasses and was wrapped in a sort of imitation of an aviator's jacket with straps and zippers and a hood.

She dug cigarettes out of a pocket in the jacket and lit one. 'Recognise me?'

I nodded. She bore some resemblance to the skinny, strung-out kid I'd dealt with some years back but, in a way, more to her mother. Or to what her mother might have looked like at about her age which I reckoned to be somewhere around twenty-five. 'Sure, Annie. I recognise you.' I was going to say that her name had come up in a recent conversation but something trapped and desperate about her smoking stopped me.

She puffed smoke. 'Yeah, I haven't changed much. More's the fucking pity.'

'Do you need help?'

'Don't we all? No, I was in the area when those bastards heavied me. I tried to hide in the park but they flushed me out with the bloody headlights. I remembered your place. So I'm here. I can piss off in a minute if you like.'

I walked past her and put the gun away in the cupboard. 'Come through to the kitchen. I want some coffee. You?'

'Coffee, yeah, okay.'

It was bright and warm in the kitchen. Annie took off her jacket and hung it over a chair. She was wearing a clean white T-shirt with SAFE SEX lettered on it and jeans. I let the cat in and she took the tin from me and fed it. Then she sat and smoked, cat on lap, while I made the coffee. The cat seemed to like the smell of the tobacco which is perhaps why we don't get along so well.

'You're looking a bit better than when I last saw you,' I said, 'but I hear you've had some trouble.'

'Trouble. Yeah. You knew Mum died?'

'No, I didn't. I hadn't seen her around for a while. She wasn't that old, was she?'

She shook her head and gave a short, wheezy laugh. 'Died of hard work.'

No fear of that for you, I thought, but I didn't say anything. I poured the coffee and carried a mug to her where she sat so the cat wouldn't be disturbed. That's a knack cats have—being considered. I'd gone out on a long limb for Annie. Maybe she was one of the people who soak up consideration like cats.

The first sips of coffee cleared my brain. 'You look all right, Annie. Are you clean?'

She shrugged. 'Methadone programme. I'm doing all right.'

She grinned and it looked as if she was struggling to pull herself up out of quicksand. 'Could I have some sugar?'

I got it for her but her hands shook so much she almost dropped her mug; the cat stirred, feeling her agitation. She stroked it, to calm herself. 'Didn't you used to have a girlfriend around here? Blonde? Student or something?'

'She wasn't a girlfriend, she was a boarder. Friend. Now she's a married dentist with a kid.'

Annie looked around the untidy kitchen and living room. It wasn't exactly squalid but the signs of minimal maintenance were plain. 'No chick in residence, eh?'

I shook my head.

'It figures. You were always a cold bastard. Good at your job though.'

'Thanks. I have to tell you this, Annie. I met a man named Greenway and he told me you were dead.'

She nodded slowly. 'That doesn't surprise me.'

'Tell me about him.'

It came out, bit by bit, over the rest of the coffee

and a lot of cigarettes. Annie had spent some time in England, come back to Australia clean but had drifted into the smack world again. She'd struggled though.

'I was maintaining when I met Gareth,' she said.

'What's that?'

'Using, but in very small amounts and very disciplined—so many hits a week, so many no-hit days, a clean week once a month. People go on like that for years, decades, it's not so bad.'

Then she met Greenway at the clinic where she got her syringes and worked part-time as a sort of minder, baby-sitter, coffee maker. She was attracted. They had a hot affair. Then he dropped her.

'Was he an addict?' I asked.

'He acted like one.'

'What does that mean?' I spoke more sharply than I intended and she bristled.

'Fuck, I don't know. He didn't shoot it, he said he smoked and popped. I never saw him do anything but grass. But he was edgy, like I feel now when you snap like that. What's the matter with you? What did I say?'

'I'm sorry. Nothing. Tell me about what happened between you.'

'Usual thing. Lots of grass, lots of wine, lots of fucking and late night TV. That's how I came to mention you. We'd been watching some private eye movie and I told him about the time you ... handled that narc and the others at Palm Beach. He was interested in that.'

'Have you ever been in Southwood Hospital, Annie?'

'Yeah, for a while.'

'He told me that's where he met you.'

'Bloody liar. He'd lie about anything. It was after that, a good while after.'

'What was Southwood like?'

'Bloody awful. Scary.'

'In what way?'

'Every way. You should've seen some of the kids there. They picked them up in the streets. Real horror cases. I don't want to talk about it. Shit!'

'What?'

'I left my stuff with those creeps. Shit!'

'Maybe we can do something about that. Tell me about what happened with you and Greenway.'

'He was living in this place at the Cross. One day he was there and the next day he wasn't. Nobody knew where he'd gone. I went down hard. I broke my own rules—hit up every day. Then I went on the methadone.'

'What about those characters that chased you in here?'

'I was scoring in the flats down the end of your street, by the water.'

'Are you going to try maintaining again?'

'I don't know. Shit, I believed him, you know? We had a great time and I thought he was for real. Fuck it. Who cares? I'd better go.'

It was after ten o'clock by then, late enough. I made us a couple of white wines and sodas and we sat in the backyard with the drinks and the cat. I explained to her why I needed to find Greenway and she seemed to understand, although she wouldn't talk about the hospital. I asked her where she was living and it sounded like a series of couches and floors and sleeping bags.

'Did you score in the flats?'

She shook her head.

The sun and the wine relaxed her. Her hands stopped shaking. She told me a bit about her time in England. She laughed, remembering good times and perhaps not giving up hope for more. I asked her to stay for a few days and she accepted. *Might need your help to find Greenway*, I thought, but I knew I needed the company more. So now I had a junkie in the house. I also had the cat around a lot more, seeing as how it likes the smell of cigarette smoke.

6

I was shaving when I realised why I'd reacted so strongly to what Annie had said. *He acted like one.* Greenway had told me he was an actor. It was a lead of sorts. I finished shaving and went out to ask Annie some more questions. I found her on the bed in the spare room, curled up under a blanket. Her jacket was on a chair and I went through the pockets. She had about twelve dollars and some change; a driver's licence, Medicare card, cigarettes, make-up, aspirin, tissues. No key. No syringe, no heroin.

I left her a note telling her how the shower worked, how to bolt the rickety back door and where the outside key was hidden. I told her not to worry about the gas smell which has been around for years without doing any harm. I told her to make herself at home and that I'd be back later. I was trusting her with a TV, a VCR and an old stereo unit which were all insured. I took the gun with me.

I used my spare car key, promising myself to get a copy cut, and drove around the block. No sign of the red Mazda which didn't mean a thing but made me feel better. The morning was cool and clear with a promise of heat in the middle of the day. I drove to Darlinghurst where Curtain Call Casting has an office in one of those streets that has been half-blocked, declared one-way and sprouted wattle trees.

Rose Moore was at her desk poring over correspondence and sets of photographs. I let my shadow fall across the desk. Rose looked up and smiled.

'Hey, that's better. Now I can't see her double chin.'

'You're in a cruel game, Rose. Dealing in people's imperfections.'

'So are you. If you've come to hire an actor for one of your dodges again you can forget it. I nearly got the sack over that.'

She was referring to a little operation I'd mounted to discourage a standover man who was making things difficult for some reasonably respectable poker players. When he encountered me and the stuntman I'd hired through Rose the next time he dropped in, he lost interest in cards. But the stuntman's agent had heard about it and Rose had been roasted. 'I'm sorry,' I said. 'I neglected the worker's compensation angle. Life's got to be so complicated.'

Rose looked something like a gypsy with wild dark hair and big liquid eyes. She accentuated the look with eye make-up, earrings and low necked blouses. Now she lifted the neckline and looked prim. 'Not if you do your job and don't cut corners.'

I laughed. 'My job *is* cutting corners, you know that. But today all I want is a look at that casting book—the mug shots.'

'Male or female or in between?'

'Male, definitely.'

She reached behind her to a bookshelf and took down the thick volume. I perched on the edge of her desk beside a stack of glossies of a young woman with hair like Tina Turner, a mouth like Joni Mitchell and eyes like Anne Bancroft.

'What does she do?' I said.

Rose lit a cigarette and blew smoke at me. 'Anything, darling. Anything at all.'

I found him on page 139—Gareth Morgan Green-

25

way. Born London 12/2/59; arrived Australia 1971; educ. Sydney High School, NIDA; 184 cm, 75 kilos, quick change artist and magician; swims, dances, sings; plays piano and guitar.

A gaunt, dark face with hooded eyes brooded from the page. Greenway had appeared in some plays I'd never heard of, a couple of low budget films and in television shows I'd never seen. His agent was Hilary Fanshawe, 111 Roscommon Street, Woolloomooloo—a walk away.

I thanked Rose and left the office. The legitimate parking place I'd found was too good to surrender—there probably wasn't another like it in a four-kilometre radius. I walked over William Street and down the hill into the 'Loo. Jimmy Carruthers grew up there and used to eat ice cream outside the pubs while his mates were boozing. Jimmy was on his way to a world boxing title—a real one.

Then it was all narrow houses and stunted factories—blank faced buildings, mean, aggressive streets. But government money has been well spent for once; the houses have been scraped back to the sandstock bricks, the wrought iron has been restored, the tin roofs are painted. The factories have been torn down, leaving more open corners to the streets, or converted into Housing Commission flats that don't clash with the original feel of the place. Rehabilitation only goes so far; there are still winos in the park which the concrete railway bridge keeps constantly in half-shadow.

Hilary Fanshawe's office was in a narrow terrace house. The door was barely a metre from the street; there was no knocker or bell but a polished hunting horn was mounted on the wall beside the number. I pressed a button on the horn and heard a trumpeting blare inside. It was the sort of sound you didn't want to hear more than once. The door gave a click and a pleasant voice came through the horn.

'It's open. Second on the left.'

I went into a narrow passage; five long strides would have taken me to the stairs, three took me to the second door which was open. The woman who sat at the desk facing the door was huge. She wore a black T-shirt; her jowls and chins settled down near its neckband. All this flesh was pale; she had green eyes and dark auburn hair.

'Yes?' It was the same voice I'd heard through the horn but sweeter and more musical. The Garbo of voices. I felt like looking around for the speaker but the fat woman's mouth was moving. 'What can I do for you?'

'Are you Hilary Fanshawe?'

She nodded. I wanted her to speak again to hear that sound.

'My name's Hardy. I'm a private detective. I'm trying to get in touch with a client of yours.'

I held up my licence and ID photo. She waved me to a chair in the small room. There were photographs everywhere photographs could be put, also magazines and film posters. 'Bail?' she said. 'Maintenance? Loan default? I assume you're some kind of process server?'

'No. That's not much in my line. Do a lot of your clients have that kind of trouble?'

'Enough. I don't suppose it's something good then—an inheritance? I could use a client with some bread. I need investors.'

'Don't we all. No, Miss Fanshawe, I don't deal in good news much either. He came to see me and then matters became rather confused. I want to see him again to straighten things out.'

'Someone should straighten your nose out. How many times has it been broken? If you were on my books I'd list it. Can you act?'

'No. Can Gareth Greenway?'

The name hit her pretty hard. She dropped the pencil she'd been fooling with and lifted her

27

head so that some of the loose flesh around her neck tightened. 'Who?'

'You heard. Gareth Greenway, one of your clients.'

'The one that got away.'

'What?'

She sighed and the flesh slackened again. 'He could've made it, I always thought. He was really good. He lifted a couple of the things he was in from shit to hopeless.' She smiled; her teeth were as beautiful as her voice. 'That's a joke, Mr ... ?'

'Hardy, Cliff Hardy.' I think I gave my full name because I wanted to hear her say it.

'You're supposed to laugh, Cliff. God, it's a double joke really.'

'I'm sorry, you're going to have to explain it to me.'

She shrugged. 'He was good, as I say. With a bit of luck and persistence he could've got good parts, made a success. I'd have been pleased for him and pleased for me.'

'But he gave up acting?'

'Threw it in.' She smiled and showed those excellent teeth again. There was a chuckle with the smile this time. 'So that joke was on me. I hardly made a cent from him. The second joke's sort of on you.'

'How's that?'

'Gareth gave up acting to be a private detective.'

7

SHE really laughed then. The flesh on her upper body shook and quivered and tears ran from her large, green eyes. 'I'm s . . . sorry,' she said. 'It just struck me as funny. God, I'm losing my grip. You must have noticed that the phone hasn't rung and no-one's called since you arrived.'

'It hasn't been long,' I said. 'You're probably in a rough patch.'

'It's nothing but rough patches.' She wiped her face and rearranged it into something like a smile. There was a charming, witty woman in there somewhere behind the blubber. 'Ah, well, I can always go back to voice-overs.'

'Is that what you did before agenting?'

'Yes, and after acting. After I got too fat. I suppose everyone was something before. You were something before you were a private eye.'

I didn't want to get into that. I'd been a happily married organisation man; sometimes it sounded good. 'Yeah. Have you got an address for Greenway?'

'Are you going to cause him trouble?'

'He's caused himself trouble already.'

'What's he done?'

'You could call it . . . impersonating a lunatic.'

She clicked her tongue. 'Gave you a performance, huh?'

I nodded.

'Told you he was good. Impersonating a lunatic,

what a part. Well, I don't owe him anything.' She pushed her swivel chair back and swung to her left. Her hand on the file card drawer was narrow, long-fingered and white. I'd heard there were people who made a living from having their hands and feet and ears photographed. I thought maybe she could do that as well as voice-overs, but I didn't say so. She pulled out a card and read off the address, '1b Selwyn Street, wait for it—Paddington. He shared with someone. No phone. Can you imagine that? An actor with no phone? I had to send him telegrams.'

'I can't imagine a detective with no phone. D'you think he was serious about that?'

'He showed me the ad he'd put in the paper.'

'What paper?'

'The *Eastern Suburbs Herald*, I think it was. It was something like Sherlock Enquiries, no, that's not it. Greenlock Enquiries. Private. Confidential. That sort of thing. Greenlock, you see?'

'Yeah,' I said. 'Holmes. Jesus. Did the ad give the Paddington address?'

'Sorry. Don't remember.'

'When was this?'

She consulted an appointments diary on her desk. 'Three months ago. January 7.' The phone rang and she almost snatched it up. She crossed her fingers and looked at me. I crossed my fingers too. She lifted the phone. 'Fanshawe Agency. Roger, how nice. Yes, I think so. Bruno? He's available I think.'

I mouthed 'Thank you' at her; she showed the first class teeth in a wide smile and I left the office.

It was uphill from the 'Loo to Darlinghurst and I was sweating when I reached my car. I drove to Selwyn Street where there were no parking places. I circled the block without finding a space so I double-parked outside number 1b which was a tiny terrace in a row that had been crimped and cutied like a poodle. A solid knock on the door brought a response from the balcony above me.

'Yes? What is it?'

I backed out onto the footpath. A young man in a singlet and jeans was leaning over the railing. Sunlight glinted on one long, dangling earring.

'I'm looking for Gareth Greenway.'

'He's not here.'

'This is the address I have.'

'He moved out when I learned that I had it.' There was a bitter edge to his voice; he sounded like the people I used to interview who'd let their insurance lapse before the fire that wiped them out.

'What?'

'What d'you think? AIDS. Gareth's not the caring and sharing type.'

His hair and beard were dark stubble over thin, tightly stretched skin. Bones protruded around his neck and along the tops of his shoulders. He was deeply tanned but he still looked sick.

'When did he go?'

He shrugged and folded his arms. The upper parts of his arms were fleshless, thinner than the forearms. 'A couple of months back.'

'D'you know where he went?'

'No. Bondi someplace. That's all. Have you got a cigarette?'

'No. Sorry.'

'Doesn't matter.' His skull-like face went back into the gloom.

Sometimes I wish I'd get a case that would take me west, to Broken Hill. As it is, I always seem to be heading east, down to the sea. I drove to Bondi Junction where the office of the *Bondi Tribune* is located. Hilary Fanshawe thought the paper Greenway had advertised in was an Eastern Suburbs rag and it seemed likely that he'd put the ad in a few papers in that area.

Everything is new in Bondi Junction and seems to be getting newer. Some of the people are old but they look as if they belong somewhere else. I had no trouble getting permission to look through back numbers of the paper. These sorts of papers are grateful for any interest shown in them. A bright-eyed young woman took me to a room which was glass on three sides. I was the only reader and everyone who walked in the corridors on all sides looked at me. No chance of making any sly excisions.

I found the ad in the issues for the first two weeks in January. *Greenlock Enquiries—discreet & determined. Negotiable rates*. At least he didn't claim experience. I wrote down the telephone number that accompanied the ad, thanked Bright Eyes and left feeling that I'd earned lunch and possibly dinner.

I had a sandwich and coffee in the mall and then I phoned my home number. No reply. Greenway picked up his phone on the third ring.

'Greenlock Enquiries.'

There was plenty of background noise in the mall to help and I deepened my voice a bit and spoke slowly. 'Mr Greenlock, I . . . '

'No, no. My name is Greenway. Greenlock is just the name of the agency. How can I help you?'

'Mr Greenway. I have a matter. I need some help.'

'Yes. Mr . . . ?'

'Barton, Neil Barton. I'd like to see you. Are you free now?'

'I am. The address is Flat 3, 12 Curlewis Street, Bondi. Can you find that all right?'

'Is it near the beach?'

'Very near. A few doors away. My office is above a supermarket.'

'I'll find it. Thank you. Thirty minutes?'

'That'll be fine.'

I hung up feeling slightly foolish about the charade. Neil Barton was an uncle of mine, an old Digger. I hadn't seen him for twenty-five years and his name just jumped into my mind. Weird. I found myself thinking about tricks of the mind and psychiatry as I headed for Curlewis Street. I was looking forward to talking such things over with Gareth Greenway. At the back of my mind was some concern about Annie. I told myself that was foolish—she'd been handling herself in a rough world for a long time and she was a survivor, like Uncle Neil, who'd come through Tobruk and other tight spots.

Number 12 was a large groceries and fruit barn with a two-storey cream brick structure behind it. There was a side entrance flanked by four letter boxes with Greenway's number above one of them. A card was Scotch-taped to the inside of the fruit shop window at eye level: Greenlock Enquiries, G. Greenway Enquiry Agent, Unit 3. I went along beside the building to a double doorway; the doors had glass panels but they were dirty and smeared. Only one of the doors opened and that let very little light into a lino-covered lobby. Flats 1 and 2 were on this level. A flight of stairs led up into more darkness.

The stairs creaked loudly and the banister was shaky. I found a switch for one of those lights that stays on for not quite long enough to let you see what you want to see. I pressed it and got enough low-wattage light to see the door to Flat 3. The door was half open. I knocked and pushed it fully open.

'Mr Greenway?'

There was no answer. I stepped into a short, narrow passage. I could smell marijuana smoke and take-away food. Rock music was playing softly further inside. A door to a kitchenette on the left was ajar. I went through to a small living room

33

which was crowded with heavy old-fashioned furniture, a filing cabinet, a TV set and a medium-sized office desk with two chairs.

'Congratulations, Mr Hardy. You found me.'

I turned quickly. Greenway had come quietly from the kichenette; he stood in the dim hall two metres away from me and he had a gun in his hand.

8

I'D had too much walking and talking and driving to be in the mood for it. I side-stepped to make him move the gun and I jumped forward fast while he was doing it. I kicked at his right knee and swung a short, hard punch at the inside of his right forearm. I connected with both; he crumpled and yelled; the gun flew from his hand and skidded across the tattered carpet. I felt twinges of pain in my bruised and battered neck but they didn't stop me landing a solid, thumping right to Greenway's ear as he went down.

I bent and picked up the gun, a Browning Nomad .22, very light with its alloy frame but enough pistol to do the job if you could use it.

Greenway pulled himself up into a sitting position against the wall. 'That wasn't necessary,' he said. 'It isn't loaded.'

I looked at the gun. 'Why d'you say that?'

'The magazine—I checked it.'

I released the spring-loaded magazine. 'Yeah, but there's one in the chamber. One's enough.'

His eyes widened. 'God. I didn't know.'

I squatted down in front of him and tapped the barrel of the gun on his knee. 'You don't seem so brain damaged now, Mr Greenway.'

'Be . . . be careful with that.'

'The safety's on now. I think it's time we had a little talk.'

I helped him up and he hobbled to a chair. I pulled

out the comfortable-looking chair from behind the desk and sat opposite him about a metre away. He rubbed his knee with his right hand; that hurt his forearm so he stopped rubbing.

'You really worked me over,' he said.

I bent my head and moved it stiffly. 'Know what? I took a first class rabbit killer from one of the hospital guards. We're not quite even yet.'

'How did you find me? I mean, I'm glad you did but . . . '

I put the Nomad on the desk and swung it around so that the muzzle pointed at his chest. 'Me first, mate. What's this all about? Why did you come to me with that phony story and the phony job?'

He grinned. 'Took you in, didn't I? With the lobotomy act?'

'I'm getting impatient. This gun's probably illegal and Dr Smith at the hospital wants to throw the book at you. You could be in serious trouble.'

'It wasn't a phony job. It isn't. I've got a client. Look, I got into this game a few months ago. I've handled a few small things—down around the lost dog level, you know? It must have been the same for you when you were starting.'

I looked at him; he had a good tan; he was wearing loose white cotton pants and a striped shirt; it wasn't warm in the dark flat but he was sweating. I didn't say anything.

'Well, this was the first real job. I didn't think I could handle it on my own and I'd heard about you so I thought I'd enlist your help.'

'Thanks a lot. So far I've been coshed and had my licence threatened. I'm really enjoying your case.'

'You've had five hundred dollars too.'

'How much have you had?'

'Two thousand.'

The mention of the money seemed to give him confidence. He eased out of his chair. 'I want a drink.

I've got some beer in the kitchen. How about you?'

'Okay. But don't get any ideas about pissing off. You're an easy man to find.'

He walked unsteadily down the passage to the kitchen and came back with two cans of Reschs Pilsener. He popped the cans and handed me one. 'How did you find me?'

I took a sip and told him in as few words as I could manage. I felt I needed to watch and listen to him a bit more before deciding what to do. He nodded, apparently respectfully.

'Pretty good. I thought you might be that good. I was giving you a test.'

'Shit, you've got a nerve. Okay, cut the charm. Let's hear about your client.'

'I haven't met him, it's all been done by telephone. He wanted photographs of that set of inmates at the hospital. The ones who exercise at that time. It seemed like a two man job to me, so I . . . '

I waved the beer can. 'Don't go into that. I might shove this down your throat. Did he say why he wanted the pictures?'

'No. He sent me the money though. Cash. I needed it.'

'If you've got any brains at all you must have known it was fishy.'

'Haven't you ever done anything fishy? Especially at the beginning? How did you get started?'

I could remember enough fishy things not to want to go on with that subject. 'I had contacts,' I grunted. 'From when I worked in insurance.'

Greenway tipped back his head and poured down most of the can. 'So did I. Actors. I was hired to beat up a guy and get a girl stoned and willing. I was hired to steal a script.'

'Did you take the jobs?'

'I tried for the script. I got the wrong one.'

We both laughed. 'One time I . . . ' I stopped. I

didn't want to get into comic reminiscences. I put the beer can on the desk next to the gun. 'Go on.'

He shrugged. 'I was desperate for something ... real. Otherwise I'd have to give this away, like I have with writing, acting ... everything. So I got the photos. I'm supposed to get another thousand when I hand them over but I haven't been contacted yet. What d'you think I should do?'

'What's the voice on the phone like?'

'Muffled. Obviously disguised.'

'Who told you where to break through the fence and when to do it?'

'He did. My client. Look, this is a few weeks ago. I didn't do anything for a while. I thought it over even after the money arrived. Then I checked on the place—went out there, talked to a girl who'd been ... '

'Annie Parker.'

That startled him. 'Right. How'd you know? You're better at this than I thought.'

'No I'm not. She came to see me this morning. She needed somewhere to duck into for a bit. Why'd you drop her? She took it hard.'

He said he was sorry but he didn't look it. 'She was a junkie. She'd been on the street in her time. I was scared of AIDS.'

'So you pissed off, like from Selwyn Street.'

He crumpled the empty beer can. 'You don't know what it's like! People wasting away around you, dying.'

'Especially if you're bi?'

'Yeah.' Something about the way he spoke the word told me he was lying. He was a master liar but there was something showing just then. The tough, selfish facade showed a crack.

'You and Annie could've had a test. Checked yourselves out. Why didn't you try that?'

The crack opened; he rubbed his eyes and pushed back his hair. Suddenly he looked older, less vain.

'Annie had the test. She was okay. I was too scared to have it. Still am. I pissed off because I was scared that if I showed up positive . . . well, I could lie and maybe give it to Annie. If I told the truth she'd drop me, wouldn't she?'

'Maybe not. Anyway, you might be clear.'

'I've been around, Mr Hardy. Want another beer?'

'Why not?'

He brought the cans and we sat drinking and not talking. I was thinking: *Life had got more complicated since the time when we worried about VD. My two cases of crabs seemed laughable. They were talking about condoms again. If I'd had to invent a brand name for condoms it'd be Fiasco. Try Fiasco condoms, you'll never . . .*

'Are you going to talk to this Dr Smith?' Greenway said suddenly. 'To get yourself off the hook?'

'No, not yet at least. You're not quite the arsehole you pretend to be. You're in trouble and you've paid me for a couple of days. I can stick with it for a bit.'

'Doing what?'

'Doing the things you should have done. Finding out a bit more about the hospital. That's the first thing.'

'What else should I have done?'

'Talked to Annie. Where's your phone?'

It was in the bedroom. I sat on the bed and dialled my number. Greenway stood, long and tense in the shadow by the door. After many rings the phone was picked up.

'Annie? It's Hardy.' I heard a groan and a sigh, sounds of despair.

'Annie?'

'What's wrong?' Greenway said.

I hushed him with a sharp movement of my hand. 'Annie!'

'I can't,' she whispered. 'I can't . . . ' There was a crash and another groan and then a long, deep silence.

9

I cut the call off and immediately dialled for an ambulance. I gave them the address and the details. I mentioned the doorkey but told them to kick the door in if they had to. I dropped the receiver and moved towards the passage.

Greenway made as if to block my path but he thought better of it and stepped aside. 'Wait. I'll come too.'

I didn't wait. I charged straight out and headed down the stairs; I could hear Greenway behind me. He caught up by the time I reached the car and I let him in. I lost seconds fumbling for the unfamiliar spare key and I swore about it.

'What?' Greenway said.

'Never mind.' I started the car and revved it savagely. 'What were you doing back there?'

He buckled on his seat belt. 'Putting the phone on record in case he calls.'

That was grace under pressure I supposed, or just cold-bloodedness. I concentrated on driving, took some chances and made good time on the freeway and down through Surry Hills to Central Railway. Greenway sat quietly. He ran his hands through his longish hair a few times and betrayed the sort of agitation that he'd suppressed on our first meeting.

'Have you got the gun?' I asked him.

'No. Think we'll need it?'

I let the 'we' pass. 'No.'

'How did she sound?'

'You know her better than me. She sounded more stoned than she could cope with.'

'God. That.'

I made myself unpopular with other drivers down Broadway and Glebe Point Road. The ambulance was standing outside my house when we arrived. The white coats moved around on the footpath and I could see my neighbours' faces at their fences and windows. I stopped in the middle of the street and walked to my gate. One of the ambulance guys held the gate closed against me.

'I live here,' I said. 'I called you.'

'Mr Hardy?'

'That's right.'

He wrote something on a sheet of paper attached to a clipboard. 'Is the young woman a relation?'

'No, a friend. How is she?'

'I'm afraid she's dead, sir. The police're on their way.'

I was aware of Greenway standing behind me. The Bondi colour had drained from his face. I drew him away towards the car. 'Can you drive?'

'Yes, of course.'

'Okay. Just park the car down the street a bit, put the keys in the glove box and get lost. There's no need for you to be part of this. I'll get in touch with you as soon as I can.' I gripped his arm and propelled him towards the car trying to look like someone giving and receiving support. 'No fancy ideas either. Just do as I say!'

He nodded, got into the car, started it and edged forward. I went back to the house and no one stopped me from going inside. Annie was lying on the floor in the living room. The telephone, with the receiver off, was buzzing beside her head. She was wearing my towelling dressing gown and nothing else. The dressing gown had fallen open revealing her pubic hair and one small pale breast. Her hair was wet. The right sleeve of the dressing gown was pushed and rolled up almost to the shoulder. There was an indentation and bruise in the soft flesh above the elbow and a puncture mark in the taut skin just below the crook of her arm.

She'd showered and scrubbed her face. With no make-up and the strain gone, with her wet hair drawn back she looked innocent, like one of the young swimming champions of the fifties. I looked at her and tried to figure out how old she was. Twenty something, not twenty-five, not that much.

The cops found the syringe and sachet in the bathroom along with the belt that had been used as a ligature. They put these things in plastic bags and also bagged all the contents of Annie's pockets. They put her clothes in a bag and they put her in a bag too and took her away. I gave them a statement: when I'd first met Annie and how; why she was in my house; what she'd said. I gave them as much of the truth as I could and they appeared to believe me selectively.

The detective in charge, a heavy, thorough type named Simmonds, asked me if there had been any heroin in the house when I'd left it that morning.

'No,' I said.

'How can you be sure?'

'I didn't have any and neither did she. I searched her stuff while she was asleep.'

'So she went out and scored?'

'Or someone came by.'

'Which?'

'I don't know.'

His shrug said it all: another dead junkie, who cares? Just as long as she doesn't have a famous name—as long as she doesn't sing or dance or act and isn't somebody important's wife or daughter. Annie was none of those things. Simmonds didn't give me a hard time.

But it's one thing to walk into a strange house and find a dead junkie and look for the quickest way to file and forget it and another to try to read the signs of what really happened. There were damp patches down the hallway to the front door but none beside the spare bed upstairs where Annie had dumped her clothes. The belt that had bit into her upper arm was hers. Annie had gone to the door after having her shower but she hadn't taken the belt from her pants unless she'd done it before she went to the door. Why would she? She didn't have any smack.

So someone had given her the smack and fetched the belt for her. A friend? Some friend. I wasn't well up on the price of heroin and it really didn't matter because from the quick look I'd got at the money the police had bagged it seemed that Annie's twelve bucks were intact. I was sifting this through when there was a loud knock on the door. Feeling ridiculous, I got the .38 from its hiding place and went to the door. The outline through the misted glass panel was long and slope-shouldered.

'Greenway?'

'Yes.'

I opened the door. 'I thought I told you to piss off.'

'I did.' He shouldered past me. He was wearing a light cotton jacket over his striped shirt and I could see a bulge in the pocket. The Nomad, no doubt. I waved him on and we went through to the living and eating space at the back of the house.

'I saw them take her out,' he said.

'Yeah? Then what did you do?'

'I caught a cab home. He called. I've got his voice on tape.'

10

GREENWAY brandished the tape and looked around. He noted the phone, with its receiver replaced but obviously not in its usual place on the bench. He put the tape in his pocket.

'Where was she?' he said.

I pointed.

'The word in the street was accidental overdose. Is that right?'

'No. At least not without some help.'

We went through to the kitchen which was dim now that the afternoon sun was low in the west. Greenway leaned against the sink while I made coffee. 'Was Annie ... what happened to her, connected to this other business?'

'Your case, you mean?'

He nodded.

'I don't know. Do you? I see you're carrying your gun. Does that mean you've got some ideas?'

He shook his head.

'No,' I said. 'Guns usually mean no ideas. Have some coffee and let's hear the tape.'

The voice was slow and deep; the background noise was an intermittent hum: *When I can talk to you in person I'll give you instructions for the delivery of the photographs.*

We played it through five times. I drank two cups of coffee. Greenway kept glancing at the place where Annie had died as if he wanted to see her there and bring her back to life. 'I thought of changing my message,' he said, 'leaving something specifically for him. But I decided that was being too clever.'

'Good. You were right. Same voice, no difference?'

'The same. Can you make anything of the background noise?'

'That's for the movies. I haven't got voiceprinting apparatus either and I can't tell a southern Hungarian accent from a Romanian.'

'I'm sorry. I know it's a mess. I didn't know what I was doing.'

I felt guilty for the sarcasm. 'All right. It happens. We have to work out what to do. Where to look for him.' I got a bottle of brandy which Helen had left behind. It was from her husband's tiny vineyard, Chateau Helene, and it wasn't bad. I put a shot in my third and Greenway's second cup of coffee. It was after four o'clock; that's late enough when there's been a death or a birth or a marriage or a horse has won or lost. I felt like working on the bottle itself, Greenway sipped moodily; booze wasn't one of his problems.

'Have you ever had a phone call from someone who seems to know you but you've never heard of them?' I said. 'Just a quick call that leaves you puzzled about how the caller got on to you or even got your number?'

'Mm, I suppose.'

'This is a bit like that. You have to sit down and build up a story that hangs together. Like—well, he must've known so-and-so and got my number that way.'

Greenway grunted, unimpressed. I finished my coffee and poured some more brandy into the cup. I added the few drops of coffee that were left. 'That's what we have to do,' I said. 'If we assume whoever hired you got to Annie somehow and killed her, or helped, how could that be? What circumstances make that possible?'

45

We both stared at the walls for a while. Greenway sighed; I drank my spiked coffee.

Greenway shrugged. 'I'm sorry. Nothing comes.'

'Try this: Mr X was watching you from the minute he made the approach. He saw you come to me, saw us go to the hospital and followed me back here. Then he saw Annie come here. He'd seen you and Annie in company before and figured she must . . . '

'Must what?'

'It gets harder here. Must . . . know something, or have seen something. So he waited until I left and made a move. He used the smack to talk his way in.'

'Well, it fits,' Greenway said slowly. 'But where does it get us?'

'If we knew what he wanted from Annie we'd be on our way. Assuming it's about the hospital, did she tell you a lot about the place?'

'Not much. She didn't like talking about it. I just checked on the routines a bit, you know. That was all I wanted.' Suddenly he straightened up from the slump he'd been sitting in. The look of tiredness and semi-shock left him.

'What is it?' I said.

'Annie kept a diary! She said she could look in her diary when I asked her about something, some little thing. I said it didn't matter.'

'It matters now,' I said.

Annie had arrived without bag or baggage and she certainly hadn't had a diary on her. So she'd left it, presumably with what she'd called her 'stuff' with 'those creeps'. All I knew was that she'd tried to score in 'the flats' and some hoods in a red Mazda had given her a bad time. I told this to Greenway who nodded. 'There's a source in those flats down by the water. What's her name?' He snapped his fingers in the first theatrical gesture I'd seen from him since our first meeting when he was doing nothing else but. 'Barbara-Ann. She's got a straight front as a caterer but she deals in a pretty big way.'

'I wonder if she's got a red Mazda,' I said.

'I wouldn't know.' Greenway adjusted his jacket. 'Why don't we go and find out?'

I had a vision of Greenway breaking in a door and waving his Nomad with the one shell in the chamber and the safety catch on. 'I'll go,' I said. 'You've got other things to do.'

'Like what?'

'You're going home to wait for the phone call. You're also going to keep a very close watch on your own back. If you're still being observed you might be able to observe the observer. That'd be a help.'

One part of him didn't like it, wanted to be in on the gung-ho stuff; the other part wanted to play it safe. I helped him out by saying that I didn't expect any excitement, just a quiet talk. He knew which part of the big complex Barbara-Ann lived in but not the precise number of her apartment. I told him I could manage and sent him back to Bondi with a promise to call when I knew anything. I wanted to take the Nomad from him but I didn't; he was confused and green, but he had some pride.

I went out into the street, collected the keys from the glove box of my car and locked it. I strolled around the neighbourhood; I got some looks from people who'd seen the ambulance and one enquiry. I didn't tell the enquirer anything she didn't know already. It was after five, the air was cooling and the TV sets were being switched on and the drinks were being poured. I walked to the open section before the road dips down into the blocks of flats and stood looking across the water towards Pyrmont. The water was still; the light faded. I moved quickly into the shelter of the trees that fringe the walkway

47

around the water and scanned the landscape behind and above me. I saw no flashes of spectacles, no quick movements. I waited; no car engines started, no birds broke cover and wheeled about in the evening sky.

11

I went home, fed the cat and myself and waited until dark. I wore sneakers, pants that were a bit big so that I needed a belt to keep them up, and a loose sweater. The .38 went inside the waist of the trousers, under the belt. I walked down to the flats where lights were burning in most of the windows. I moved through the parking areas on to the concrete path that wound between the different blocks. Some of the windows on to the balconies were open; rock music and television made a confusing mixture of conflicting sound.

The phone book had supplied the lacking information. In the sections for caterers there was a small ad: 'Barbara-Ann, Home Catering, small functions, Apartment 5, Block 3, Harbourside, Ludwig Street, Glebe.' The place was in one of the better locations, high enough to command a good look at the water and with its fair share of waving trees to shut out the less salubrious views. The parking bay allotted to Apartment 5 held a red Mazda coupe.

There was no point in being subtle about it. No reason to throw pebbles at windows or climb up the ivy on to the balcony. There was no ivy anyway, and the balcony to Apartment 5 was ten metres up. I went through the glass door into the lobby and climbed the stairs. I knocked at Number 2. A middle-aged man in a cummerbund and dress shirt came to the door and said his name wasn't Williams and that he didn't know any Williamses in the block.

I thanked him after getting a good look at the security chain: not much good—a heavy shoulder, properly delivered, would tear it from the frame. I hoped my stiff neck wouldn't hold me back. Up another flight to Number 5; I listened at the door—music and talk. I smelled marijuana smoke. Hardy, with all senses on the alert.

I took out the gun and held it low and out of sight. I knocked and pressed my ear to the door. The occupants didn't fall silent or start cocking machine guns. The door opened ten centimetres and I saw a small woman with a mass of curling, red-gold hair.

'Barbara-Ann?' I said.

Her pupils were dilated and her eyes were red the way some pot smokers' get. 'Mmm,' she said.

I hit the door with everything I had. The chain tore out and the door flew open whacking her in the knee and hip. She staggered back and I bullocked through the opening. I grabbed her by the arm and dragged her down the short passage to a living room with a white carpet, white leather and chrome fittings and air like at a NORML smoke-in. There were two men in the room, stoned and slow-reacting. One wore his shirt collar turned up. He was the pale-faced driver of the Mazda.

'Hey, what's this?' he said.

I shoved the woman into one of the white chairs and stood behind her. She swivelled around to look at me. That made three pairs of eyes focussing on the .38. Paleface was half out of his seat; I waved him back down. The other, a flabby-faced kid, dropped the fat, smoking joint on the carpet.

'You'd better pick that up or you'll have a nasty burn there,' I said. He bent slowly and recovered the cigarette.

'We don't want any trouble,' the woman said.

'Neither do I.' I moved around and stood to one side from where I could have shot any one of them except that none was moving a muscle.

50

'I know you,' Paleface said.

'You've seen me. I wouldn't call it a relationship.'

'Who is he?' The woman was recovering fast; she was slim and lean, like a gymnast, about thirty and with small, hard eyes behind which a lot of fast thinking was going on.

'My name's Hardy, Barbara-Ann. I was a friend of Annie Parker. I'm here to invite you all to her funeral.'

'We don't know anything about that,' Paleface said.

'Shut up, Vic,' Barbara-Ann said.

'No, I want to hear about it. I want to hear about how you took her some smack and she OD'd on it. I want to know why.'

'We didn't ... we didn't!' The kid's voice was shrill. 'You saw us drive off. We didn't come back. We just ... '

'That'll do then,' I said. 'You just what?'

'Watched your joint.'

'And what did you see?'

Barbara-Ann and Paleface Vic both looked at the kid. He found some courage among the fear somewhere and clamped his jaw. Barbara-Ann stirred in her chair.

'You can just fuck off, whoever you are,' she said. 'You've got no business here.'

'I'm a Federal policeman, Barbara-Ann. I've got business everywhere.'

'See!' The kid yelped as the burning joint singed his fingers. He dropped it on the glass-topped table. 'She was with the narcs. We told you!'

Barbara-Ann and Paleface looked at me trying to make up their minds. I didn't want them to do too much thinking. 'It's the girl I'm interested in,' I said. 'Not you lot. I'll settle for two things—what she left behind her here and what you saw when you were watching my house.'

Barbara-Ann drew in a deep breath and tossed

back her cascade of phony-coloured hair. 'Then you'll go?'

'That's right.'

'What the fuck do I care? Lyle, get the bag she left.'

The kid got up and scurried out of the room. He came back quickly with a canvas bag. I kept my eyes on Paleface and gestured with the gun for Lyle to open the bag. 'Let's see what's in it.'

Barbara-Ann reached for the bag of grass on the table. 'We haven't touched it.'

Lyle pulled out a shirt and some underpants. He stuffed them back and produced two paperbacks and a thick exercise book. Paleface was bracing himself. I told Lyle to put the books back and do up the straps. He did it and I reached for the bag, looped it over my shoulder. I was getting tired of standing up and watching people who didn't like me. Barbara-Ann rolled a joint.

'Okay, make it quick,' I said. 'What did you see? Hold off on lighting that, Babs, until we're finished.' I lifted the gun a fraction, aware that its effect was wearing off.

Lyle was the only one still scared. 'We saw a guy arrive and go to the door. She let him in.'

'What sort of a guy?'

'Just a guy. You know.'

'I *don't* know. Young, old, tall, short, thin, fat? What sort of car did he drive?'

Paleface didn't like being left out of things. He took the joint from Barbara-Ann, lit it and expelled smoke slowly. 'A white Volvo. Middle-aged man, like you. Medium everything except for his hair.' He ran his hand through his own lank, straggly locks, took another drag and handed the joint to the woman. 'A baldy, with a thick moustache instead. The way baldies do.'

'Okay.' The bag was slipping from my shoulder

and I shrugged it back up. Paleface must've thought this was the time to move. He came up from his chair bent low and ready to club my gun hand down. He was much too slow; I had time to step back and watch him lose balance as his move misfired. I hit him with the back of my hand along the side of his narrow, bony jaw. I felt the shock around the grip of the gun but he felt it more. He groaned and crumpled. A spurt of blood from his nose sprayed and smeared over the white carpet.

'Now look what you've done,' I said. 'That'll cost a lot to clean.'

Paleface rolled over on to his back. His eyes were fierce but wet; he sniffed back a nose full of blood. I stepped around him and stood beside Barbara-Ann.

'Just for that,' I said, 'I get another question. Annie was here to score. Did she say anything interesting? Share any thoughts with you?'

'She was hanging out.' Barbara-Ann drew on the joint. 'She had no bread and she tried to con us. That's it.'

'You're a lovely person.' I put the gun in my belt and walked out. I could smell the marijuana smoke all the way down the stairs and I heard two high-pitched yells and a slap before I was out in the fresh air.

12

I had a white Volvo, a bald man with a thick moustache and an exercise book diary. Not a bad night's work. All I needed was a drink and a feeling that I could make some sense of Greenway's crazy, mixed-up case.

I went home and took the drink out on to the balcony for a while. I sat and watched the street. No red Mazda, no skulking figures or firebombers. I wasn't surprised; they'd probably moved up to something heavier than the grass and were on the way to feeling that they were clever and brave and everything was all right.

I cleared a space on the bench beside the phone, switched on the reading lamp and opened Annie Parker's diary. Someone said that historians are people who read other people's letters. I've never done any historical research but I've read a few private letters and I understand the attraction. A sort of fly-on-the-wall feeling with a touch of taboo. Reading a private diary was much the same. Annie made half page entries, never missing a day. The diary began in the early part of the previous year and stopped two days before she died.

I flicked over the pages, just getting impressions at first. Adults who write a lot or take notes acquire bad habits—personal shorthands and squiggles that mean zero to anyone else. Or they take to typewriters and word processors and almost forget how to write by hand. Annie's writing was neat and clear, a regular script without quirks, like that of a mature child. I remembered that she'd had a good school record before she went wild.

She kept a simple record of what she'd done, who she'd seen and how she felt. The entries were brief with the identities of people concealed: *Saw C.A. and scored. Went to Bondi. Heavily hassled by L. who's splitting (he says) for Bali. Wanted me to go with him. No thanks. Feeling better about F.* She was concerned about her weight: *48 k. Not bad.* And her health: *Saw Dr Charley and got a prescription for antibiotic. No drinking for three days.*

Greenway was 'G.'. The entries confirmed what she'd told me—that they'd met at a drug clinic and clicked. She knew he was bisexual. For the time they were together the entries were brief and mostly positive: *G. is a fantastic fucker and talker and I'm not real bad myself when I get going.* Trouble started between them over the AIDS test. She couldn't understand 'G.'s reluctance to have it. Then he disappeared. The entries after the breakup were black: *Slept all day. Hanging out. Methadone is murder.*

I turned back to her record of her period in Southwood Hospital. *Have to hide this,* she wrote. *No diary keeping allowed. Fuck them!* Things didn't improve. She had nothing good to say for the staff or the treatment but she liked some of her fellow patients: *M.Mc. is a sweetie and he's brilliant! Nothing wrong with him. What about A.P.?* The writing became crabbed and hasty: *Long, creepy interview with Dr S. today. No programme. No way!* One entry was tear-stained: *M.Mc. was done today. He's finished. No-one home.* A few days later the letters 'E.F.', 'J. O'B.' and 'R.R.' were encircled. Then, the day before she left the hospital she recorded: *M.Mc., E.F., J.O'B. & R.R. have been transferred (they say).*

The process by which Annie got out of the hospital was a little hard to follow through the maze of initials and other abbreviations. It happened a few weeks after 'J.O'B.' and the others were 'transferred'. It seemed that a new member of the staff, a 'Dr K.', had helped her to secure a certificate of detoxification. A solicitor had done the rest. While in the hospital Annie had read a lot: *The Brothers K.*, *W & P.*, *The I. of Dreams*. She had come out resolved to find 'M.Mc.' but there was no sign that she'd done anything about it. She was 'maintaining' and working at the clinic when she met 'G.'.

It wasn't hard to make a certain amount of sense out of it. Something was happening at the hospital that Annie was afraid of, wanted no part of. There appeared to be victims. It half-fitted with Greenway's story of being hired by someone who was concerned about one of the patients. But that story had been an invention; he now said that he had knowledge of the motives of his hirer who was taking his time in collecting what he'd paid so much money for. It all got back to that—who hired Greenway and why?

I phoned him and got the answering machine. I read some more of the diary without gaining further enlightenment except into the character of Annie. She had lived day to day, without plans until she'd met Greenway. They'd discussed the future, something Annie had refused to do for years. That made it all the harder for her when, suddenly, there was no future anymore. She went back to recording and living her life in small, safe units. Except they weren't safe. Police and pushers cropped up through the entries and they were sometimes one and the same.

She'd started the diary the day after her mother died as some sort of comfort for the loss. She talked to her sister and brother at the funeral and spoke lovingly of them. I didn't recall the siblings but I had a clear recollection of the mother—a stout, strong-minded Cockney who'd never understood why Annie had got on to drugs but had never stopped caring about her, even though she'd suffered the usual thefts and let-downs.

In the pages that covered the time with Greenway Annie had made small sketches, post stamp size. There was a reasonable likeness of Greenway, some flowers, a few other faces. The sketches were happy. Her spelling wasn't perfect but neither is mine. I felt I was getting closer to her and I felt a mounting anger at her death and the manner of it. There were more than a hundred pages blank in the exercise book. She was someone who'd taken bad knocks and had tried not to go under. She should have had those days and a hell of a lot more besides.

I phoned Greenway again and this time he answered in a harsh, broken whisper.

'What's wrong with you?' I said.

'Can you get over to my place, Hardy?' he rasped. 'He was here. He drugged me and he's taken the fucking photographs.'

13

I'D had enough for one day. I got Greenway calmed down, established that he wasn't injured and told him that we had some other leads.

'What leads?'

'I've got the diary.'

'Jesus, that's great! Bring it over.'

'Forget it. I've got fifteen years on you and I need some sleep.'

'Sleep! I couldn't sleep.'

'Yes, you can. Take a long walk. Take a pill. I'll be over in the morning.'

'No, Hardy, you can't . . .'

'I can. Listen, if your brain needs something to work on try this.' I read him off my list of initials. 'Chew on them. See if they mean anything to you.'

I finally got him off the line. I checked the doors and windows, wedged a chair in against the back door that won't lock properly, and went to bed. My neck was still sore from the rabbit punch and my hand ached from the blow I'd given Paleface. They were the physical sufferings; I was still feeling bad about Annie. A lot of people had let her down and maybe I was one of them. Maybe I should have stayed with her. Bad thoughts. I had her diary under my pillow along with the .38 but it didn't give me any bad dreams. I slept heavily, no dreams at all.

Greenway answered the door looking like a man who hadn't slept for a week. His hair was tousled, his stubble was long and his eyes were red. He smelt bad too.

'Go and have a shower,' I said. 'I'll make some coffee. I can't talk to anyone who looks that bad, you remind me of myself when I was twenty-five.'

Greenway grinned. 'Well, you made it to fifty.'

'I'm not ... You stink, and change your shirt.'

I made instant coffee in the kitchenette and prowled around the small flat. Greenway had spent some of his sleepless night cleaning up and the place didn't look too bad. There was a slight smell in the bedroom and I located the source—a thick gauze pad which had been soaked in ether. Greenway had put it in a plastic bag the way he'd seen it done in the movies. I also located a large manilla envelope which had been sealed with masking tape and torn open. I had exhibits one and two on the table with the coffee when he came out, showered and shaved and in a clean T-shirt. He nodded and put three spoonsful of sugar in his coffee.

'He was waiting for me.'

'You put up much of a fight?'

'Not much. God, he was strong and I was a bit pissed. I had a few on the way home. The photos were made into the bed, at the bottom. I thought it was pretty smart but he must've found them in no time.'

'How long were you out to it?'

'Not long. Half an hour, bit less.'

'Nothing else taken or disturbed?'

He shook his head and drank some of his coffee syrup. 'Have you got the diary with you?'

'Let's stay with this for a minute. You didn't get a look at him, sense anything, smell anything?'

'No. All I smelled was the ether. All I can tell you about him was that he must be heavy and strong. I've seldom ... '

'What?'

He waved his hand in one of his rare theatrical gestures. 'Well, I've been in close contact with a few men, if you see what I mean. Not many as strong as this guy.'

'Okay. Did you notice anything when you got home?'

'Like what?'

'Lights on, doors open, cars parked?'

He drank some more coffee and made an effort to remember. 'N ... no. There was a car across the road I don't remember seeing before. I noticed because it was so clean.'

'What kind?'

'I don't know about cars. No idea.'

'What colour?'

'White.'

I grunted. 'Anything else?'

'Don't think so. Oh, hold on.' He lifted his hand and brushed it against his ear. 'I felt something before I went under. Something against my ear. Hair. I'd say he had a moustache. There's something else too ... but I can't quite get it.'

'That's good enough.'

'How is it good?'

I told him about the man with the heavy moustache and the white Volvo who'd been let into my house by Annie. He opened his eyes in surprise and then winced as too much Bondi sunlight hit them. I handed him the diary. 'Did those initials mean anything to you?'

'I heard Annie talk about someone she called Obie, could've been this O'B., but I don't know.'

'First name?'

'No idea. Sorry. She said he was very smart, smarter than me. Something bad happened to him but I don't know what.'

'Read the entries for the time she was in hospital.

You'd better not look at what she wrote after you dropped her. You might think less well of yourself.'

While he read I phoned Frank Parker in Homicide for information on Annie Parker. He got a summary of the medical examiner's report and proceeded to be cautious.

'What d'you want to know?'

'Cause of death.'

'Narcotics overdose. Death through respiratory and cardiac failure.'

'Heroin?'

'No, morphine. How would you classify this death, Cliff?'

'Probably an accident.'

'I don't think we have a category "accident—probably"; what about something more definite?'

'Accident then.'

'Nothing in it for me?'

'Don't think so.' Frank said something about Hilde and his baby son which I didn't hear because I wasn't listening. My mind was running somewhere else. *Morphine and ether. A white Volvo.* Sounded like a doctor to me. 'Hold on, Frank. Maybe you might be interested in this. I can't tell you much now . . .'

'But you want me to tell you something.'

'Right. The Southwood Hospital in Sutherland. Might you have something on it?'

'We might. I might have time to look. You might call me, eh?'

'Thanks, Frank. Good about Hilde and the kid.'

'I told you they had measles, you prick.'

I squeezed out of that somehow. When I put the phone down Greenway was closing the diary. He got a crumpled, much-used tissue out of his pocket and wiped his eyes. 'Shit,' he said.

'Are you talking about yourself?'

61

'You didn't do such a great job either.'

'Right. I feel like making some kind of amends, what about you?'

'What can we do?'

'We can break about five laws and take a look at the records of Southwood Hospital.'

62

14

GREENWAY made more coffee and we drank
that and then started on beer. I gave him my doctor
theory and we looked through Annie's diary for
medicos. We came upon 'Dr Charley', the druggies'
friend, whom Greenway knew.

'Not him,' he said. 'He's out of his brain himself
most of the time.'

We got 'Dr S.' and 'Dr K.' from the diary. S.
would be Smith whom I'd met. K. meant nothing to
either of us. Greenway began prowling the room
restlessly. 'How about checking the registration records to see if a doctor at the hospital has a white
Volvo?' he said.

'That'd be harder than you think. Most doctors
are incorporated these days, their cars are registered to their companies. Or they lease them. It'd
be easier to go and look in the car park.'

'Well?'

'Yeah, maybe, but would you go to work in a car
you'd used the way that Volvo was used yesterday?
I wouldn't.'

'Hey!' He dug around in a pile of newspapers on a
chair, bent and looked on the floor. 'Shit!'

'What?'

'He took my gun!'

'Great! Well, it could be worse. It only had one
shell in it.'

'No. I loaded the full clip at home yesterday.'

I shook my head. 'Well, it's not so bad. We're

looking for a strong, bald doctor with a white Volvo, a fully loaded Browning Nomad and a thick moustache.'

Greenway shook his head slowly. I looked at him enquiringly. 'I dunno about the moustache. I've remembered what I was trying to recall before. From acting—I smelled that spirit gum you use to stick on false beards and moustaches.'

I gave him a small round of applause. 'Terrific recall. And I've just thought of something else.'

'What?'

'It could've been used to stick down a bald wig.'

We both laughed.

Greenway was exhausted from his long day and sleepless night. He sank lower in his chair and his eyes kept closing and I had to tell him to go to bed.

'What're you going to do?'

'Make telephone calls. Really run up a bill. We're still using this bastard's money, aren't we?'

He yawned. 'Suppose so. Okay, I'll snatch an hour.'

Within ten minutes he was sleeping deeply, looked like he'd be out for six hours at least. I left a note in case I was wrong and drove to my office in St Peter's Lane. That was a waste of petrol and effort. Nothing there needing attention. No lonely clients with Rita Hayworth legs. Even Primo Tomasetti the tattooist, with whom I could usually waste some time, was on holidays and his establishment was closed. I knew why I was there of course—to check the mail and the answering machine for messages from Helen. I didn't know whether I wanted a message or not, but there was nothing.

Back in Bondi, I bought a late lunch—two big salad sandwiches—and a six pack in Campbell Parade and ate one sandwich and drank one can sitting on the grass and looking out to sea. It was fine and warm with a clear sky and a pollution-clearing breeze. When I was young I'd come here to surf. Now they came to score—and surf, probably. It was confusing. I examined the big painting on a signboard which showed what the redevelopment of the foreshore would look like—park, playground, pavilion. It didn't look any different which was fine by me; I like Bondi the way it is.

Greenway was still asleep. I'd shaken the cans a bit and the one I opened in the kitchen sprayed. I swore and dropped another can. Greenway woke up and came stumbling into the kitchen. I handed him the frothing can.

'Brunch,' I said.

'Great.' He lifted the dripping can and took a long pull. I examined him while he was drinking; he was tanned and lean, almost thin but not unhealthy looking. I pointed to the sandwich on the kitchen table and he fell on it. If he was carrying the AIDS germ it hadn't done any damage yet to his appetite or powers of recovery.

He munched and spoke around the lettuce and carrot. 'Well, what now?'

'You go to the clinic where you met Annie. Ask around. See if anyone was asking for her, or you. Try your description of your assailant on people.'

'Description? Assailant?'

'Improvise. Do your best. Wouldn't be a computer buff, would you? I looked around but you don't seem to have equipped yourself with a PC yet.'

'I know a bit about them,' he said huffily. 'I can get by. Why?'

'The hospital's records are all on computer. It occurred to me the safe way to do it would be to break into the system. We could sit in comfort while a hacker found out all we wanted to know.'

He snorted. 'That's in the movies. It's more complicated than that. You have to know the codes.

You'd have to work on the hospital's system first. Comes to the same thing—a break in.'

I opened a can carefully and waited for the foam to rise gently through the hole. 'I feared as much. The old ways are always best,' I said.

Greenway left and I phoned Ian Sangster who is my friend and personal physician, also sometime tennis partner and drinking companion. I asked him what he knew about Southwood Hospital.

'Not a lot. Nothing really good.'

'Anything really bad?'

'No.'

'How hard would it be to identify a doctor who works or worked there just from his initial?'

'First or last initial?'

'Don't know.'

'Jesus Christ, Cliff! What're you playing at? There's some very disturbed people at Southwood.'

'How hard, Ian?'

'Bloody near impossible. One of the things about the place that's not quite . . . you know, kosher, is the turnover of medical staff. Pretty big.'

'Who's the money behind it?'

'I've heard rumours but I'd rather not say—not over the phone to a person of dubious reputation.'

I was going to tell him that I wasn't using my own phone and then I remembered that Greenway fell into the same category, sort of. I thanked him and hung up. The day was wearing on; I had a choice between another beer and a walk. I took the walk, trying to get out of the lengthening shadows into the afternoon sun. I thought about women—Helen and Annie and Cyn and others. All different, all difficult, all more interesting to think about than men.

I called Frank from a public phone.

'What's all that noise behind you?' he said.

'From the street. I'm using a public phone for

security. No private phone is safe in the late eighties.'

'Bullshit. Still, might be just as well.'

'What've you got on the hospital?'

'Nothing solid. The word is some of the staff need rehabilitating as much as the patients.'

'Meaning?'

'Southwood has been known to give people a second chance.'

'I see. Anything known about the financial set-up?'

His voice seemed to drop but it might have been my imagination. 'Various sources. But a large medical practice with numerous . . . branches, is not unconnected.'

'That's interesting.'

'Watch your step, Cliff. They've got lawyers . . . '

'I'd never do anything against the law, Frank. You know that.'

15

DRIVING south with Greenway the second time was a very different experience from the first. He was alert, anxious to talk, and he seemed to think we had a good deal to talk about. First, he had to tell me about the success of his mission to the clinic.

'I'm sure it's the same guy,' he said. 'Thickset, bald, asking about Annie.' He consulted his notebook. 'Time's a bit vague—a few weeks ago maybe.'

'Doctor? White Volvo?'

'Not known.'

'Cut it out. You're right though, it sounds like a piece of the puzzle.'

I'd seen one of the hospital's computer terminals and he questioned me closely about it. Had I the make of computer and the model? Was there a printer attached? Did I see a photocopier? I wasn't much help. With regard to Smith's office I mostly remembered my aching head and the single malt.

He rubbed at some dirt on the windscreen. 'Not very observant, are you?'

'At least I didn't get my gun stolen.' It was a silly reply but it shut him up long enough for me to brief him on what we needed from the records: names corresponding to the initials in Annie's diary and everything to do with them; a 'Dr K.' if possible; evidence on the hospital's finances; drug irregularities.

Greenway nodded. 'Anything else?'

'Yeah. Anything that seems relevant.'

I questioned him about the hospital's security arrangements which he'd observed on a preliminary visit, before he roped me in.

'I didn't see any patrols or anything like that. I don't think there's a resident security man. I think some kind of security service paid a couple of calls.'

'You *think*?'

'They did. Once or twice. I was pretty tired.'

'That means a good alarm system. Could be tricky. How many patients and live-in staff, would you say?'

He thought about it for a kilometre or so. 'Thirty-five patients, round about. The administrator's got a flat in the grounds and there're nurses on duty around the clock.'

'Male nurses?'

'I think . . . yes, I saw one.'

'There's your night-time security man. We'll have to handle him somehow. Any ideas, Greenway?'

'Call me Gareth.'

'I can't call anyone Gareth. How about Greenie?'

'Jesus. Well, what about a diversion?'

'You're learning.'

It was a dark night, no moon and Southwood Hospital didn't go in for floodlighting. There were lights on some of the buildings and along sections of path that were used at night, but most of the place was in deep darkness. I drove past the front entrance and up a side street looking for high ground. We found it in a quiet street on the south side of the hospital. We sat in the car and pooled our knowledge about the layout.

'How do we do it?' Greenwood's voice almost broke. He was nervous. I didn't feel a hundred per cent confident myself.

'We can go through the fence. It wasn't wired before, no reason to think it would be now. I

69

assume the buildings have alarms—doors and windows and such.'

'You could set off an alarm in one of the buildings while I go for the administration building.'

'I could. With a bit of luck I can disconnect the alarm before you go in. I've got the tools. If it's not too complicated.'

'That's it then.'

'You'll need some time. We might need something to keep them busy for a while.'

'Like what?'

'Let's not think too far ahead. We can't anticipate what might happen.'

I got my burglar kit, packed into a soft airline bag, from the back of the car and checked the items. Metal things that might clink were wrapped. We cut the fence and moved down the slopes carefully, skirting the pools of light, until we reached the main buildings. It was after ten, late for a hospital where activity begins early. We checked Smith's flat; a light was on and classical music was playing softly. We waited until the music stopped and the light went out. It was quiet in the wards; from a hiding place behind bushes near the spot where our charge of a couple of days back had ended, we could see dim lights, some movement, but the hatches were battened down.

'Time to go.' We bent and scuttled across to the long, low administration block. The alarm system was an infra red, magic eye job. I located the wiring and traced it to a point where I could work on the circuits. I had to freeze once and crouch behind scanty cover when a big man in nurse's starched whites came out of the adjacent building for a smoke. Luckily, he smoked fast and didn't look around. I immobilised the alarm and used a skeleton key on a side door.

'You know what to look for.' I held Greenway's

arm and hissed in his ear. 'Be as quick and quiet as you can. Try to shade any light you have to use. I'll set an alarm off if you need cover. Ignore it. I'll set off another one if it looks like you're spotted. That's when you get out. I'll meet you by the toilet block.'

He slipped into the building. I moved around the grounds willing everything to stay quiet. I could hear the soft pounding of the sea; a light wind moved the tops of the trees. Edgy and alert, I heard every bird call and dog bark; a ship hooted far away to the east. Nothing moved in the hospital grounds. I stationed myself by the alarm of one of the buildings near the swimming pool and squinted down to the administration block. Greenway had had about half an hour. A faint light showed in a window that should have been dark. The light moved. I swore.

My swearing seemed to act as a signal. The male nurse I'd seen before came out of the north wing and checked his watch. He looked around and saw the light. I broke the circuit and the alarm shrilled above me. The nurse came out again, this time with another man I recognised as the rabbit killer expert. I ducked back and moved across to a second building. They ran towards me. I broke another magic eye beam and a second alarm joined in with a high-pitched wail.

I tried to focus on the door, willing Greenway to come out but he didn't. I could hear the two men running, not far away now. I was near the swimming pool where there was no cover. If they looked in the right direction they'd see me. I looked down the slope again and saw a red winking light. The high main gate was suddenly caught in the full beam of a patrol car's headlights. Lights came on around the swimming pool; I was standing at the deep end, plainly visible in dark clothes in the eerie green light.

'Hey, you!' The rabbit puncher rushed towards me. His name was stencilled on the pocket of his starched uniform shirt—POPE. I ran around the edge of the pool. He came after me, quick and eager. I tripped on something made of metal and he was on me. He had short arms and came in pumping hard, clubbing punches. I ducked under a clumsy haymaker and punched him hard and low. He gasped and let go with a roundhouse swing that would have taken my head off. I rammed him in the groin with my tool bag and he screamed and fell.

More lights were coming on and I could hear shouts. I still couldn't see any sign of Greenway. Then I saw what had tripped me—a can of petrol standing beside a motor mower. A plastic oil can sat in the grass catcher. I grabbed the cans, unscrewed their lids and splashed them out into the swimming pool. I heard a groan and a protest from Pope. He was crawling along the edge of the pool towards me.

'Get away!' I had matches in the tool bag. I groped for them, lit five or six together. The man rolled off to his left as I threw the blazing matches into the pool. There was a roar and a sheet of flame leapt five metres in the air and danced across the lapping water.

16

I ran away from the intense heat and light into the
darkness, working my way towards the meeting
point with Greenway. There was a lot of noise—men
and women shouting and one of the alarms was still
ringing. I heard glass break. Ahead I saw a flash of
white and a crouched, fast moving figure.

'Greenway?'

'Here.' He was carrying a bundle of paper, struggling to keep the flapping sheets under control.
'What the hell did you do?'

'Later. Let's go!'

We raced up the slope towards our exit in the
fence. I sneaked a look back before we scrambled
through: the fire was dying down in the swimming
pool; the front gate was open and the patrol car had
pulled up in front of Smith's flat. Lights were on
everywhere—in the flat, in the wards and in the
administration building.

We were both panting when we reached the car.
Lights showed in some of the houses; shapes moved
at windows. No time to hang about. I threw the
bag into the car and gunned the motor. Greenway
clutched his paper to his chest as we took off fast,
the way the old Falcon never would.

We travelled a few minutes in silence. The eye I'd
damaged a few years back that sometimes gave me
trouble when I was under stress was aching now and
watering. I slowed down. 'There's a flask of rum in
the tool bag,' I said. 'Let's have a drink.'

Greenway gave me first swig and then took one himself. 'We did it!' he said. 'What was burning?'

'The swimming pool. You don't think I'd set fire to a hospital, do you? Did you find out what we wanted?'

'Some of it. I haven't exactly had time to analyse it thoroughly ... ' He giggled and took another drink.

'Okay. We don't want you going into shock. Calm down.' I could feel him glaring at me as I drove and I realised that the sarcasm was my expression of relief. I reached across for the rum. 'We'll stop somewhere soon and take a look. You did pretty well.'

He was glad to be mollified. 'So did you. Some diversion.'

'Yeah. I hope nobody got hurt. Have another small swig.'

We stopped at a take-away chicken place wedged in between the car yards in Kirrawee. I bought some chicken and Coca Cola and took it to one of the two tables. The tired-looking girl serving eyed me suspiciously. She pushed back her orange-dyed hair and rested her hip against the counter. 'How long youse goin' to be?'

'Why?' I said.

'I'm closin' up in twenny minutes.'

'That's long enough.' I realised I was hungry. I ate the chicken and sipped the Coca Cola, after I'd put rum in it. Greenway was sorting papers. He ate some chicken; he had natural good manners and was careful not to get grease on the sheets. 'What did you get?'

'The patients are or were, Michael McCleod, Renee Riatoli, Eddy Forster and John O'Brien.'

'Why were they there?'

'Drugs.'

'What? Drugs!' The girl looked sharply at us

and checked her watch. I dropped my voice. 'Drug problems and they were operated on?'

'That's what it looks like. There's a lot of psychology stuff—depression and all that, but when you boil it down . . . '

'Shit! Where are they now?'

He shrugged. 'Don't know. I didn't have much time and getting into some of the files was complicated. They sort of . . . exited the filing system. The codes're a bit difficult to follow. I printed some of it out. I tell you, the printer sounded like a machine gun in there.'

'What about the staff and the money angle?'

'Nothing on the money. It'd have taken all night to get into that. The staff stuff's strange, man. It's as if files are being kept on them too, like the patients. Some of it's stuff they wouldn't like everyone to know. Kinky . . . '

'Spare me. Is there a doctor with "K" in his name?'

'Several. Some of the files are hard copy, I mean paper. The personnel stuff has photographs, good ones.'

'That'd be in filing cabinets. How'd you handle that?'

'In for a penny in for a pound. I jemmied them with a metal ruler. I took a chance and used the Xerox machine.'

'That must've been the light I saw.'

'There was no way to shield it.'

Greenway drank, and ate some more chicken; he licked his fingers and I noticed that his hands were steady. He'd handled himself very coolly throughout. 'It doesn't matter now,' I said. 'Let's see the pictures.'

He arranged them on the table. I glanced at the seven faces quickly and then examined each in turn closely. I held up the third. Greenway nodded.

'Dr Bruce Krey. He fits physically. Bald, see. No moustache but look at his shoulders. And his personal file's a beauty. He's had a fair bit of treatment over the years. Boy, does he have problems. I copied a fair bit of his file, didn't bother with the others. Hardy?'

I was scarcely listening. The face was that of the doctor who'd examined me as I was regaining consciousness at the hospital on day one. His bald head had been covered then by some kind of cap. I'd misheard his name as 'Grey'.

Greenway was looking pleased with himself. 'Here's the trump card. Shit, where is it?' He shuffled the papers frantically.

'Closin' time,' the girl called.

'Christ, I can't find it!'

I stood and collected the papers. 'Take it easy. It'll be there. This kid's shagged, she wants to knock off.' I left two dollars under the chicken tray and the girl gave me a smile as we went out the door. In the car I used a torch to help Greenway locate what he wanted. A single photocopy sheet.

'It was on the boss's desk,' he said. 'Look. Krey resigned today.'

17

KREY'S address was given in his file—25 Seventh Street, Jannali. I checked the directory, started the car and headed back up the Princes Highway. Greenway didn't speak and I was happy to be left with my own thoughts. The intelligence that Krey was our man posed a lot of questions. 'Dr K.' was one of Annie's good guys—he'd helped her get out of Southwood. So why was he an apparent instrument of her death? And why had he hired Greenway to do something that made no sense, especially when he was on the spot in the hospital himself? Just knowing Krey was a source of trouble took us no closer to knowing what the real trouble was and what had killed Annie.

Greenway coughed. 'I don't want to look nerdish or anything, but isn't it something for the police?'

I concentrated on not missing the turn-off. My eye was still watering and I dabbed at it. 'How would you like to explain what we did at the hospital?'

'We're investigating a crime, a series of crimes.'

'What crimes?'

'Murder for one and . . . '

'Accidental death.'

'Assault.'

'On who?'

'Me.'

I laughed. 'You're a bisexual out-of-work actor playing at being a detective. You've never even met your client. You've got no protection. Are you bonded?'

'What's that?'

'Insured against damage you might cause, losses that might be sustained through your actions.'

'No.'

'I'm told this hospital has million dollar lawyers, the kind that own racehorses. You'd be so up to your balls in writs you'd forget what this was all about.'

He rubbed his hand across his face. 'Yes,' he said wearily. 'You're right. What *is* it all about, anyway?'

I made the turn. 'We'll go and ask Dr Krey. Let's hope he's home.'

The road into Jannali wound around the natural features of the landscape. There seemed to be a lot of roadworks going on devoted to changing those features. The suburb was quiet, like a country town all closed down for the night. I drove through unfamiliar streets with big houses contending for the high ground to the down-market section where the planners seemd to have run out of names. I wondered what it would be like to have as your address No. 1 First Street, or No. 2 Second Street for that matter. Seventh Street was undistinguishable from the others—widely spaced fibro bungalows on standard sized blocks. It was short and dark; several of the street lights were out of commission.

'Not much for a doctor,' Greenway said. 'Looks like the sort of place they dump defectors in—where nothing happens and nobody goes.'

He was right; the street wore an air of uniformity and dullness that didn't seem to fit with the personality of Dr Krey as I remembered him. I recalled the vein bulging in his forehead and the sense of pressure building up in him like an overheated boiler. I imagined him living in a penthouse or a slum, not low-rent suburbia. I drove slowly past the house; no lights were showing but the tail end of a big white car protruded from the driveway on to the wide grassy strip—the street had no footpath.

Greenway leaned across me and squinted into the gloom. 'Could be a Volvo.'

'It is.' I drove on to the end of the street and parked. Most of the houses had garages or carports but there were a few cars on the grass strip—kids' bombs mostly but a few sedate sedans like mine.

I dabbed at my eye, found a torch in the tool bag and got out of the car. 'You wait here.'

'No!'

'Shut up! D'you want people calling the cops? This is a nervous neighbourhood. You have to stay here to guard the documents and to give me a warning if anyone comes. Two honks, okay?'

'Bullshit, no one'll come.'

'Just do as I say.'

I closed the car door quietly and walked along the grass. Although my footsteps were silent a few dogs growled in the backyards and some lights indicated late night movie watchers but I had the street to myself. I examined the car at No. 20. The Volvo was heavily laden with boxes, bundles and cases. Dr Krey was planning a trip. I moved cautiously towards the house. I could see now that there was a light at the back. I went into the garage and used my torch to locate its back door. This opened on to a bare patch with a trellis gate through to the backyard. No dog.

The house was quiet and I had a feeling that it was empty, the way you get a feeling after a few rings that no one is going to answer the phone. I've had the feeling often; sometimes I've been right and sometimes wrong. I had it once and walked in on three dead bodies. I tried the back door and it opened easily and quietly. That took me into a porch; the door to the kitchen was open. One light burned and the stove was warm. There was an oil heater with a red light glowing in the dark living room. I looked quickly into the two bedrooms, using the torch. Both empty and more or less stripped. One had been used as a study but all that was left were some newspapers. I stood in the front room smelling loneliness, frustration and fear. I moved the torch beam around carefully and saw something on the ledge above the built-in electric fire. I touched it and felt hard bristles and a soft backing—a false moustache.

Two honks sounded from the street. I switched off the torch and went to the window. Through the gap beside the blind I saw a burly man approach the house. He rested his hand proprietorially on the Volvo as he eased past it. Krey. He walked towards the front of the house. I took the .38 from my belt and held it at my side. I heard Krey's footsteps on the path.

Two honks again, longer this time and louder. More company.

18

I couldn't see Krey now, he was too close to the house, but I saw his visitor—he wasn't wearing his uniform whites anymore but, even in the badly lit street, I couldn't mistake him—Pope, the rabbit killer. He seemed not to notice the car horn; he stood behind the Volvo, lifted his arm and levelled a pistol at Krey's back.

I whipped up the blind and smashed the window. I yelled something and brought my gun out. Pope swore and fired. The bullet whanged into the door. I stuck my head out trying to get a better look and saw Krey crouched behind a bush near the front door. Pope's attention was divided between his target and me.

'Pope!' I pointed the .38 at him. 'Drop the gun.'

Pope hesitated. There were two sharp reports; the windscreen of the Volvo shattered and Pope screamed and reeled back. His gun flew in the air and he collapsed in a heap. Krey remained in a crouch; he held Greenway's short-barrelled Nomad, still pointing it at the car.

'Dr Krey, put the gun down.' It's hard to achieve much authority speaking through a broken window and Krey ignored me. I moved across the room, through the passage and opened the front door. He was crouched four or five metres away now; he'd jumped like a rabbit towards the corner of the garage. His eyes were wide and staring; he saw me step from the house and he raised the gun.

'Don't shoot,' I said. 'No more shooting.'

Greenway appeared beside the car. 'He's got my gun.' He looked down. 'This man's dead, I think.'

Krey moaned and moved the gun.

'Doctor, stay calm. I'm a witness. Self defence.'

Krey raised the gun and rested it with the muzzle on his right temple.

'No, Krey. Don't!'

He stood stiffly and moved into the shadows, just inside the garage. The shots had brought people to their doors and gates. Noise was building in the street. Someone ran across the road and bent over Pope.

'Greenway,' I said. 'Try to keep those people back. Tell someone to call the police.' I tried to keep my voice low and unalarming but I could hear Krey moving, shuffling back further into the darkness. 'I'm going to try to talk to him.'

'Don't come in!' The voice was sharp and clear.

'I won't, doctor, don't worry. There'll be some people to help here soon.'

'I'm beyond help, Hardy.'

'That's not true. Tell me about it. You hired Greenway, did you?'

He laughed softly. 'You've got a pretty good therapist's voice, Hardy, but it won't do any good. Yes, I hired him. I knew something rotten was going on at Southwood.'

'Operating on drug abuse patients?'

'Yes. Smith—trying to make a name for himself, going after American research grants. Barbaric!'

'Easy. Why didn't you make a report, go through the proper channels?'

He didn't reply and I edged forward to the corner of the garage. 'I can hear you,' he snapped. 'Stay there! No one would believe me. I've got a record of . . . instability.'

'What about Greenway?'

'It wasn't a very clever thing to do. I hired him to cause trouble. I thought Smith might make some sort of mistake.'

'You were acting when you and Smith interviewed me? After Pope had knocked me out.'

'Acting? Yes, yes.'

He sounded edgy as hell; I had to keep pushing him but it was hard to know how hard to push. 'Annie Parker,' I said softly. 'You helped her get out of Southwood.'

'I'm sorry about the girl. I lost track of her after she left the hospital. Then I followed you home and she turned up. I didn't mean to hurt her. The morphine was too pure or ... I don't know. Something went wrong.'

'What did she tell you?'

'The patients are dead.'

'Did she tell you that?'

'She brought me to see it!' His voice rose and shook. 'They were guinea pigs! That thug Pope picked them up and brought them in like Jews to Belsen. They're dead. I know it.'

'Perhaps you're right.' I heard cars in the street but thankfully no sirens. People were moving around and some of the voices carried to me. I hoped they didn't reach Krey. I could feel waves of fear and despair coming from him through the darkness. 'So you got the photographs back from Greenway and resigned your post. Look, it's not so bad. You can get clear of this. The girl thought well of you; I've got her diary ... '

'Don't tell me that. I killed her.'

'Come out. Let's talk properly.'

'You still don't see it, do you?'

'See what?'

'They'll blame me. It'll come out and they'll blame me.'

'How can they? You had nothing to do with it.'

'They've got lawyers. They can do anything. That's why I was going to kill him.' The voice was soft, barely audible.

'Kill who?'

'Smith. I took a taxi. I went ... to the hospital. No, I stopped the taxi and came back. I'm confused.'

'Yes, you are, Dr Krey. Please put the gun down and come out. It'll be all right.'

'No. Stay back. That was Pope, wasn't it? I see it now. Smith sent him to kill me.'

'Perhaps he did. That's in your favour.' There was movement behind me; I looked and saw two uniformed policemen approaching with their weapons drawn. I waved them back. 'There'll be an enquiry. Smith is in trouble.'

'Enquiry, Oh God, no. No, not another enquiry. I couldn't stand that.'

'Doctor ...!'

The shot from the Browning was loud and sharp like ten stockwhips cracking at once. I bent low and moved into the garage. The torch beam swept across the oil-stained concrete slab and stopped on Krey's face. He was on his back, eyes open; his head had fallen to the right a little so no wound was visible but the eyes were still and sightless.

19

THE cops rushed in and were reluctant to listen to my explanations. They had wanted to alert the Tactical Response Force and were angry that it wasn't necessary. One of them escorted me from the garage back to the street where Greenway was backed up against the Volvo. A big cop was practically standing on his feet he was sticking so close to him. Greenway was in shock or very nearly; he was pale and he seemed to have aged ten years. They took my gun away.

Two police cars roared into the street, swung on to the grass and braked centimetres from Krey's neighbour's fence. The constables got in some practice at crowd control. It was the most excitement Seventh Street had ever seen and everybody turned out. A hot dog seller could have done very well. I got cold standing around and was short-tempered when a detective arrived to take charge. He ignored everybody while he looked at bodies and guns. Then he listened to the most articulate of the uniformed men.

He nodded. 'Bag them,' he said. 'Get these two to town. Don't be rough.'

'That's because he respects our civil rights,' I said to Greenway who needed cheering up.

The detective lit a cigarette. 'I couldn't give a shit about your civil rights, Hardy,' he said. He waved the cigarette at a van pulling up across the street. 'The TV boys've arrived. I wouldn't want them to get the wrong impression.' He squared his shoulders, straightened his tie and took a last drag on his smoke. He'd stubbed it out when a blonde reporter with cabaret makeup, a trench coat and spike heels shoved a microphone under his nose.

'Could you give us a statement, please.' She smiled winningly for the camera and the cop.

'Yes. We received a report . . . '

I turned away and dived into the back of the nearest car. The last thing I need in my game is TV pictures of me being taken in for questioning. Greenway was right behind me; he seemed to have forgotten his former profession.

They took us to the new police headquarters, gave us coffee and brought in a smooth talking type to take statements and sniff the air. Greenway wanted to go back to day one but he tied himself in knots within a few sentences. I didn't say anything.

'Mr Hardy?' Smoothie said.

'I think we should give our accounts separately. I also think my lawyer should be here. He could represent us both.'

Greenway protested. 'I can't afford . . . '

'You can't afford not to,' I said. 'Sackville—here's the number.'

Smoothie nodded. He wasn't like a cop at all. 'Very wise,' he said.

It took a long time for them to find Cy Sackville and nothing could keep Greenway quiet. When he mentioned the hospital I glared at him.

'Don't worry, Hardy,' Smoothie said. 'We've got the documents from your car. We can put two and two together.'

'I hope so,' I said. 'There's a lot more than two and two in this.'

Sackville arrived; we made statements and were charged with trespass, illegal entry, arson and burglary. Greenway was charged with possession of an unlicensed firearm. Sackville tried to get us out that night but it was no go. We were held in the headquarters lockup, went before the magistrate in Glebe in the morning and were given bail.

When we walked out of the court Greenway and I were unshaven and rumpled. Sackville was his usual dapper self. Frank Parker was waiting in the sunshine. We shook hands. He nodded to Greenway and Sackville.

'I told you to be careful,' he said.

'I was. Now tell me about Southwood Hospital.'

'We paid a visit. Dr Smith got very confused about this bloke Pope. He made some damaging admissions.'

'This won't come to trial,' Sackville said. 'I'm rather sorry in a way.'

'How's that?' I said. 'You hate courts, hate and fear 'em.'

'True. But I would've liked to see how the prosecution handled the matter of arson of a swimming pool.'

Like most things in life, I never came to a full understanding of it. Dr Krey wasn't the most rational of individuals and his movements and motives in regard to his hiring and watching of Greenway, his surveillance of my house and some of his other thought processes could only be guessed at. Investigations showed he had a record of intellectual brilliance and emotional instability. Some years back he'd been at the centre of an investigation into radical drug-based techniques for relieving anxiety and depression. He'd come out of the investigation with major financial and personality damage.

Legal proceedings over Smith and Southwood Hospital became very involved. Smith was charged with conspiracy to murder Dr Krey but there was insufficient evidence to sustain the charge. Greenway and I concluded that Smith must have connected Krey with our raid on the hospital, but no one seemed very interested. The hospital's records had been confiscated but Smith had destroyed or removed some of them in the hours between our break-in and the arrival of the police.

'That was a terrible job,' Frank told me. 'You should've made the records secure. It's a dog's breakfast now.'

'I had other things on my mind. That Pope was a dangerous type.'

'Yeah. Doc Krey got off a lucky shot. Pope'd been shot before and he'd done some shooting. He was a hard case. Southwood had a few of them. And dodgy doctors. A real shithole.'

We were having this conversation in Hyde Park, eating sandwiches and trying to stay warm on a bench in a patch of sunlight on a cold May day. I flipped a crust at a seagull with pleasant markings and watched sourly while another bird got it first. 'What about the patients who went missing?'

Parker shrugged. 'Dead is my guess. You know how many people pop off in New South Wales every year?'

'No idea.'

'Over forty thousand. It's a big deck to shuffle and Smith'd be just the boy to shuffle it.'

'Krey said he found out something about them from Annie Parker. He reckoned Smith'd do anything to get into the big research grants.'

'Yeah, you told me. And Pope netted junkies like butterflies. That's not much use to us now, is it?' Frank crumpled his paper bag and threw it five metres into a bin. 'That Annie was a second cousin of mine. Didn't know that, did you?'

'No.'

'Neither did I before this. That's modern life—we've got kin we don't know about all over the place. I've probably put a few of mine away. How about your mate, Greenway? What's he doing?'

'Haven't seen him.'

Greenway phoned me a few days later. He told me he'd gone back to acting and had a part in a stage musical. It was in rehearsal. He'd get me tickets.

Helen likes musicals, I thought. 'Thanks,' I said. 'You can sing, can you?'

'And dance. And tell you what, I took the AIDS test. I'm clear.'

'Great. Now you just have to find somebody the same.'

'I've found him,' Greenway said.

Cloudburst

OLD habits are hard to kill, like old memories. I was sitting in my car waiting for a city light to change so the traffic could trickle ahead. The city fathers were experimenting with traffic arrangements to cope with the construction of the Pitt Street mall. I'm looking forward to the mall but I wasn't enjoying the stop-start motoring. It started to rain and I instinctively reached for a rag I keep as a stopper for the window where the rubber seal has rotted away. But there was no need; I was in my new Falcon that doesn't leak. That was better but not everything was better. Back when I had a leaky car I had Helen, more hopes and the traffic moved. I sat and waited, warm and dry, and remembered.

The rain had started at 6 pm on Saturday September 10 and it hadn't stopped by the following weekend. Everyone could remember the moment of the cloudburst the way you can remember what you were doing when Kerr sacked Gough. I was taking a walk to get a cup of coffee at the Bar Napoli in Leichhardt. I was halfway between home and the coffee and I decided to go on for the coffee. The rain fell as if it had been stored up there for ten years. The floor of the coffee bar was awash when I arrived and the place was crowded with people seeking shelter from the storm. We stood around and drank our coffee and looked out at the sheeting rain and agreed we'd never seen anything like it.

People kept saying it.

'I've never seen anything like it.' A week later

that's what the NRMA guy who came after a three hour wait to help me start my Falcon said.

'Yeah,' I said.

'I've never seen anything like it,' Helen Broadway said that night. Helen was with me for six months, on leave from her husband as per her arrangement with him and me. 'Have you?'

I kissed the back of her neck. 'That's what I like about you,' I said. 'You're different. Everybody's saying they've never seen anything like it—you're the first one to say "have you?"'

She turned away from the omelette she was making and looked at me. 'Well, have you?'

'Not in Sydney. I've seen it as heavy in Malaya but there it lasts for half an hour, this has been going on for what—eight days?'

'Mm. It's a funny thing, you know. I was reading that this is common in Sydney, happens every year. You all just forget about it from one year to the next.'

'Could be. We're a feckless lot.'

She put the pan under the grill and waved at me to set the table. 'This is the last of the eggs. We're going to have to go out again for provisions. You reckon the car'll start?'

'Worse than that. I'm going to have to go to the office. I need work.'

'Nobody'll want anything done in this weather.'

'They might. There might be a job for a Senior Swimming Certificate holding detective who rode the waves at Maroubra on a surfboard made of fence palings.'

'You didn't, did you?'

'So legend has it.'

'You can't go out, you haven't got any dry shoes.'

'I'll dry some tonight, wrap them in plastic, go out barefoot and put the shoes on when I'm inside. That way anyone coming to see me will know I'm smart because I've got dry shoes.'

'No one will come. You'll sit there in your dry shoes all alone when you could be in bed with me.'

Helen was wrong. I *did* have a client. She arrived within two minutes of me sitting down behind my desk and struggling into the sneakers I'd dried on top of the heater. They were stiff and cracked and didn't look good with the rest of my clothes. I was still wiggling my toes when she walked into the office. Into means into: she came through the door after a quick knock and that took her straight up to my desk. No anterooms, secretary's nooks, conversation pits for Cliff Hardy, the low rent detective with integrity and cracked sneakers.

'Come in and sit down,' I said. 'I'm glad of the company.' I peered at her through the gloom which had settled over the city and seeped into all rooms not floodlit.

'The building did seem very quiet,' she said. 'I wasn't sure it was inhabited.'

'It is and it isn't,' I said. 'What can I do for you?'

Adjusting to the murk, I could see that she was in early middle age, middle sized and middle class. She wore a wide brimmed hat and a coat of the same shiny black material that shed water. She had on a long dark skirt and black boots—a trifle funereal but functional. She took off the hat and shook out a head of blonde-streaked, mid-brown hair.

'Roberta Landy-Drake gave me your name, Mr Hardy. She said you could handle ... celebrities.'

'Did you know she was joking?'

She frowned. Her handsome face creased up and I got the idea that she'd been doing a good deal of frowning lately. 'I don't follow you.'

'I've been the chucker-out at some of her parties. I've handled celebrities, literally.'

'Oh, I see. It doesn't matter. The point is, Roberta says you don't go off selling gossip to the papers or blackmail people.'

I nodded. 'You'll have to forgive me. If you're a celebrity I'm afraid I don't know you. Maybe it's a bore but you'll have to tell me your name.'

'My name is Barbara Winslow. I'm not a celebrity but my husband is.'

'Oh, god,' I said.

Ian Winslow was the flavour of the month politician. He'd been to the right schools, had the right degree and looked good on television. What he thought was anybody's guess, what he said reflected his deep concern. He was deeply concerned about everything, particularly about ethnic affairs which was his current portfolio, but also about health and police and any other headline worthy subject you chose. To me, he seemed to care deeply for his teeth and brushing his hair boyishly.

'You don't approve of him?' Barbara Winslow said. 'I'd be surprised if you supported the other side.'

She was looking at my sneakers. Fair enough; politics is class-based or should be. My credentials were all around me—on my feet, on the pitted surface of my desk, on the windows which looked dirtier inside now that the outside had been washed and rinsed by God.

'It's not that. I just don't like having anything to do with politics . . . '

'This is a man in trouble.'

'Politicians aren't men, they're networks of obligations and enmities.'

'They have families.'

So do axe murderers, I thought. I said nothing; she stood and walked over to the window. There was so much water pounding the glass and moving on its surface that the window itself looked liquid and insubstantial. When she turned around her eyes were wet.

'You *have* to help me. Roberta said you would.'

I nodded, took a note pad from my desk and offered her a cigarette from the office packet. She refused which was wise because they were stale. But she was comforted by the gesture; she left the window and sat down again. She was eager to talk, eager to see me write, eager to pay me money.

'Ian Winslow,' I said and wrote the name in block capitals. 'By this time next year he'll probably be in charge of the department that licenses me. Self interest suggests I should help you.'

'The year after that and he could be in charge of the state.'

'Well . . . ?'

'He's behaving strangely, going out at odd times, not accounting for his movements. He's nervy and . . .'

'Off his food?'

'Roberta said you'd joke and not to mind. But this isn't a joke.'

'Okay. Politicians have a million worries; people ring them up at all hours; they have to breathe other people's air a lot.'

'I know. This is different. I want you to follow him when he goes out at night and find out what he does.'

'I could just ask one of his security boys.'

'He's called them off. He goes out alone.'

That *was* strange; politicians like a huddle—it helps absorb the egg or lead and makes them feel important. You almost never see one silhouetted against the sky like Clint Eastwood. As she put it the job didn't sound so hard. At least I wouldn't be craning to look over the heads of a lot of guys with thick waists and short haircuts. But if she wanted an early start I'd have to wear goggles and a snorkel. She began taking hundred dollar notes out of an envelope.

'I suppose you want me to start when the weather clears up.'

'I want you to start tonight.'

At 10 pm I was sitting in my car watching the exit to the car park of The Belvedere which is one of the new, tall apartment blocks they've built overlooking Darling Harbour. Eventually, when a few hundred million dollars of taxpayers' money has been spent on beautifying everything around there, the people who've spent big bucks on their apartments will have a lovely view instead of scraped earth and stained concrete. The rain hadn't let up so that for now they had acres of pale mud to look at. Tough.

I'd left Helen at home with a stack of video recordings of movies she'd missed because she lived half the year in the bush. She'd promised to keep me some wine and to hold off on 'Night Moves' until I got back. She'd keep the promise but I knew I didn't have to worry about her waiting censoriously up for me. If I got home by midnight or thereabouts, fine; if not, I could find her in the bed.

I was listening to a smart-arse radio hack being rude to his callers. The things the people who called wanted to talk about got sillier and sillier so I couldn't blame him. No one wants to do silly things—like sit in a leaking car in a rainstorm watching a hole in the ground when there's a woman and a cask and 'North by Northwest' waiting at home.

At 11 pm a white Commodore carrying the number plate Barbara Winslow had given me roared up the ramp. It barely paused at the footpath and swung right past me with indicator lights blinking brightly through the steady rain. I started the

Falcon, indicated right as I pulled away from the kerb, and kept the indicators flashing as I followed the Commodore. We drove east, past the dark, silent department stores and the bottomless mine shafts they're sinking as part of the renovation of the Queen Victoria Building.

The rubbers on the Falcon's windscreen wipers weren't new and they didn't do a good job on the clean water falling from the sky or the dirty stuff being splashed up from the road. I had to squint, rub the glass and drive closer to the Commodore than I would have liked. I'd caught a glimpse of the driver when the car first appeared and I could see the line of his head and shoulders as we sloshed through the city. It was Winslow all right, fair hair, chin up and no slouching.

We went up through Taylor Square, skirted Paddington and swished into those streets near Trumper Park where the kids would be odds on not to know who the park commemorated. The Commodore turned into a street lined with Moreton Bay fig trees. The rain had stripped a lot of the leaves and left them as mush in the gutters and on the road but there was enough foliage left to hood the street lights already dimmed by rain. Nothing wrong with the Commodore's stop lights though; they flashed at me bright and early enough to allow me to drop back and pull in to the kerb well before Winslow parked.

Ignoring the rain, I wound down the window to get a clearer view as Winslow flicked the car door closed and scooted through a gate to a deep verandah running the width of a well-kept, double-fronted terrace house. Winslow shook water from his light rain coat by flapping it and jerking his shoulders. He looked nervous as he knocked. A light came on over his head and a woman appeared in the doorway. Winslow grabbed her as if his life depended on trapping her where she stood. Her slender bare arms wrapped around him and I could see her face before she buried it in his shoulder: black hair gleamed under the porch light; teeth and eyes shone against a skin the colour of a ripe plum.

The light went out and with it a sour breath from me. Peeper Hardy strikes again. I waited long enough to be sure he wasn't just there to hand out a How to Vote card and then I drove home. The water was over the hubcaps in several places between Woollahra and Glebe, and the rain fell hard all night. I drank wine and watched Gene Hackman and went to bed with Helen and didn't hear the rain. Somehow I thought Ian Winslow wouldn't be hearing it either.

'Poor woman,' Helen said as she buttered the toast. The rain had stopped but big, black clouds hung over the city. We had the lights on at nine o'clock in the morning.

'Which one?' I said.

'The wife.' She passed me the toast and I poured coffee for us both.

'What about the other one?'

'Hmm. He's the Minister for Ethnic Affairs, isn't he? God, it's like that Shirley Maclaine joke about Peacock. He was the Minister for Foreign Affairs so I gave him one to remember.' She bit into her toast, dropped crumbs on her silk dressing gown and brushed them on to the floor. 'I don't find Shirley Maclaine all that funny, do you?'

I shook my head. 'I don't find Peacock all that funny either.'

'He's funny compared with Fraser.'

'It's raining again,' I said.

'What're you going to do?'

'Take another look at the place.'

'What good will that do?' Helen pushed her chair

back and reached for her packet of Gitanes. She smoked one a day, sometimes first thing in the morning, sometimes last thing at night. You could never tell which it would be. She didn't know herself.

'Hardy's law,' I said. 'Put off doing an unpleasant thing if you can. Something worse might happen and then the first thing won't look so bad.'

Helen smiled and lit her cigarette.

I'd wasted most of the morning waiting for the rain to stop. It didn't, so now it was early in the afternoon and I'd been watching the house in Woollahra for an hour. In that time I'd seen four women. One was the person who'd greeted Ian Winslow so enthusiastically the night before. She looked even more exotic in the daytime. She'd run down to the corner shop when the rain stopped briefly. She moved like a dancer, long legs, lithe body in tights and a loose sweater. Her hair was piled up on her head like a high, black turban revealing a long, slender neck circled by a white ribbon. Another of the women, who also ran a short errand, was almost as dark but had a different cast to her features, less African, more Indian. The other two were Asian or Eurasian, possibly Filipino. Dressed for the wet weather, they left in taxis.

On a dry day I'd have felt conspicuous. The other cars in the street were younger and better bred than mine; the houses all had that heavily mortgaged but well cared-for look, and there was no soggy rubbish in the gutters like in Glebe. It wasn't a place for loitering in. I had my hand on the ignition key when the door of the house flew open and a woman ran out on to the street. She threw her head back and screamed up at the leaking sky as she ran. A man charged out of the house but was checked by a passing car. The woman ran down the footpath towards me, still screaming, bare feet flying and one arm flopping oddly as she moved. I got out of the car and she almost fell into my arms. The blood on her rubbed off on me. The man came on; he was dark and big but flabby. There was blood on his white shirt. He stopped and the three of us stood there in the rain.

'Come,' the man said. He beckoned with an impatient flick of his fingers.

The woman shivered and shrank closer to me.

'She doesn't want to come,' I said. 'Why don't you go?'

'Wife,' he said.

'No! No!' She gripped my arm. Blood dripped on to the wet footpath. He reached for her and I stepped forward and chopped at the muscle of his extended arm. He yelped and swung at me but he had to move his feet to do it. One foot came down on some Moreton Bay mush and he started to slip; I helped him with a shove to the shoulder. He slithered and crashed into the side of a car. His leg twisted under him as he went down hard.

The woman was small and light; I half-carried her to my car, pushed her across to the passenger side and got behind the wheel. As we turned the corner out of the street I looked in the rear vision mirror—the dark man was lurching across the road towards the house and the African Queen was rushing out into the rain to meet him.

'You need a doctor.' Blood was welling up from a slash across her right forearm; her left arm was giving her pain. She winced as she tried to straighten it.

'Yes.' Her voice was just above a whisper, hard to hear with the noise of my old engine, old wipers and the hiss of traffic on a wet road. She was young and pretty with delicate features and a pale amber skin. Her black hair had been held up by combs one of which had fallen out so that she had a half disordered look that would have been very attractive if it weren't for the blood and the trembling spasms that shook her. Her thin dress was soaked.

A kilometre from the Woollahra house, I pulled up outside one of the twenty-four-hour clinics that have sprung up around the city in recent times. She glanced out the window and shrieked. Her hands clutched for a hold on the dashboard.

'No, no, not here! No!'

Jesus, what is this? I thought, but I got moving again.

'Okay, okay, I'll get you to my doctor. All right?'

She nodded and slumped down in the seat. When I could spare attention from the treacherous roads I glanced across at her. She wasn't dead and she wasn't asleep—half-alive would about describe it.

Ian Sangster stitched the cut in the right arm and eased the dislocated shoulder back. He put the left arm in a sling. The woman took it all without a murmur.

'Bad cut, Cliff,' Ian said.

'Dangerous place, the kitchen; almost as bad as the bedroom.'

Ian sniffed. 'She's got some nasty bruises too. There was a big, strong man involved.'

'He's limping now,' I said. 'Tell me, Ian, what d'you think of these clinics—the joints with the leather lounges and cocktail cabinets?'

'A few of them're all right, some'll be video shops in six months.' He snorted. 'Come to think of it, that's about what they are now, some of 'em. Why?'

'No reason.'

'If you're sick, come to me.'

'I haven't been sick since I stopped smoking.'

'Wise, very wise.' Ian smoked fifty a day.

She gave me a name on the drive home, Lela Somosi, and told me she was a Filipino. That's all;

she was almost unconscious. Shock and exhaustion, Ian had said. I squelched up the path to the front of my house half-carrying her as before—great stuff for the neighbours. Helen let me in and didn't ask any questions. She put Lela Somosi in a warm bath, gave her a dressing gown and made her some tea. The woman clutched the mug and took a sip. She smiled at Helen.

'Thank you.'

'We'll show you where you can sleep in a minute,' I said. 'But will you tell me about that house first?'

She nodded. 'Women come there from overseas. We are not here legally. We work as prostitutes. For those who are most ... happy and the beautiful ones, it can be only three months. For others it can be six months or a year.'

'For what?' I said.

'To get papers. Real papers. Legal papers for Australia.'

'And what happened to you today?'

'I am not happy. The men do not like me. Richard tells me I will never get the papers unless I change. We fight.'

'Richard?'

'Richard da Silva, he is the boss. He is from Brazil.'

'Who's the black woman, the tall one?'

'She's tired, Cliff. Let her sleep,' Helen said.

'No. I will tell you. She is Riki Marquand, from Brazil.'

'And that doctor you wouldn't go to.'

'He does things for Richard. I thank you for helping me. I would like to know why you do it, but I am tired now.'

'It's all right,' I said. 'Have some sleep. More talk later.'

Helen took her into the spare room and I made some sandwiches and got out the flagon. I put one glass down quickly and poured two more as Helen came in.

'Saw you,' she said.

'I've earned it, wouldn't you say?'

'Mm.' She drank and took a bite of tomato and cheese. 'Your client's hubby's in the shit, isn't he?'

'Could be.'

'What do you mean? A Cabinet minister in some sleazy girl immigration racket? This has to go to the police or the Crime Authority or something.'

'Client comes first.'

'Explain.' She took a long pull on her wine and nibbled at a crust.

'I wasn't hired to blow the whistle on Winslow. I just have to report to his wife on what he's doing.'

'That's passing the buck to her. *She* won't do anything.'

I shrugged. 'If I go around reporting to the authorities on everything I find out about people no one will hire me. I'll be out of business.'

'This is different.'

'Yeah, it is. But the principle remains the same.'

'*Principle!*'

We argued it back and forth for a while, drinking wine and getting nowhere. We got heated and exasperated. At about five o'clock Helen looked out the window; there was a fitful glow in the pale sky about where the sun would be, if it ever came back.

'I'm going to a movie,' she said. '*Romancing the Stone*, want to come?'

'No thanks. D'you want the car?'

'No thanks. See you.'

She went and I wandered around the house for a while. I put the wine away and had some coffee; then I got the wine out again and had some more. I looked in on Lela—she was deeply asleep with both damaged arms lying free and looking comfortable. At seven o'clock I walked along Glebe Point Road, stretching my legs for the first time in days and thinking about food and principles. The footpath was drying out in patches and the air smelled and tasted clean. I had some food in one of the coffee shops, bought gin and Gitanes as a peace offering for Helen and came back with the same principles I'd started out with.

For some reason the gate to my place opens outwards so I always close it when I leave. As I turned into the street I could see the gate hanging over the footpath. I ran. The door to the house was open and banging against the splintered jamb. I raced up the stairs to the spare room. The bed was almost undisturbed but Lela Somosi was gone. I stood in the room blaming myself and building up a head of anger. When I got downstairs Helen had just walked in. I nodded to her, grabbed the phone and dialled Barbara Winslow's number. I was still carrying the shopping and Helen came across and took it gently from me.

'Mrs Winslow?'

'Yes.'

'This is Cliff Hardy.'

'Who?'

'Cliff Hardy. I have to talk to you.'

'You must have the wrong number.' She hung up. I looked stupidly at the receiver, shook my head and pressed the redial button. The phone rang and rang until the connection was broken by the automatic cut-off.

I stumbled out to the kitchen and watched Helen pour gin over ice. I took the glass and drank half of it in a gulp.

'Don't say it,' I snarled.

'I wasn't going to.'

'No, you wouldn't. I'm sorry, love. I've been so dumb. Bastards!'

'Have you got her cheque?'

'Cash.'

'What do you think happened?'

'Somebody's worked fast—put me in Woollahra and connected me to Winslow's wife. God knows how. Ian must've got a scare and promised her he wouldn't do it again.'

'What about Lela? . . . What are you doing?'

I was getting my Smith & Wesson and the holster from the locked drawer under the hi-fi. 'I'm going out there to get that da Silva guy. I'll bend him until he gives me the girl.'

'Go to the police.'

'I've got nothing to tell them—no witness, no evidence.'

'You're being dumb again.'

'Probably.'

I drove like a madman to Woollahra, at speeds that would've killed me and others just hours before on the wet roads. But the roads were dry now and the night sky was clear and starry. I held the gun in one hand and wrapped the other in an old sweater. I planned to go through the window and break anything else I had to on the way to da Silva. But Helen had been right. The house was dark and quiet. I let my pulse slow, put the gun back in the car and took out some picklocks instead.

Inside all that remained was a strong smell of perfume. There was no furniture, no books, no newspapers, no people. The cover-up had started and I knew how it would go on from there. The neighbours would know nothing; the estate agent would have dealt with intermediaries; the property would be owned by a company which was owned by another company and so on.

I drove to the clinic and parked outside. Now that the rain had stopped and my windows weren't misted I could see through the plate glass doors.

There was a statue inside—Michelangelo's 'David'. There was also white carpet and Scandinavian furniture—I wondered how David felt about that. Lela had said that the doctor here did things for da Silva. As I understood it, these places had a fluid casual staff. Did she mean the Boss Doctor or Doctor Smith who worked on Wednesday nights? Nothing here either.

'Nothing,' I said to Helen.

'I found this in a pocket of her dress.' She held out a scrap of paper which was still damp from the rain. On it was written 'Luis 818 2456'.

'A friend?' Helen said.

'That's what she needed.' I dialled the number.

'Yes?'

I covered the receiver. 'How d'you pronounce it?' Helen shrugged.

'Lewis?' I said.

'Yes. Who is this?'

'I'm a friend of Lela Somosi; I'd like to talk to you.'

'Is Lela there?' The voice was young, quick and excited.

'No. Can we meet?'

'You are not the police?'

'No.'

'Immigration?'

'No. I took Lela away from the house in Woollahra today.'

'Where is she?'

I drew a deep breath. 'I don't know.'

'They have taken her back?'

'I think so, yes.'

There was a sob in the voice. 'Then she is dead.' The sound of weeping, deep and racking, came over the line. I held on to the phone, feeling useless and guilty, until he composed himself. I told him what had happened. He wept again. He told me that he

105

had met Lela at the house where he had gone in the company of his boss. He named him, a union leader I had read about. Luis had tried to persuade Lela to get away from da Silva. She was afraid and had resisted. He'd written out his name and number for her.

'How do you know she's dead, Luis?'

'I know. I can show you.'

He named a place. I met him there. The rain had started again and it kept up, slashing through the dark night sky, while a quiet little Latin American showed me how murder and disposal were done, Sydney style, 1984.

The next day the harassment began. A cop stopped me and went over the Falcon with a microscope. He found the unlicensed gun and declared the car unroadworthy. I got a three month suspension of my investigator's licence for the gun. I got unpleasant phone calls and the clicks and rattles that punctuated calls I made from my home and office phones practically drowned out conversation. Winslow was showing me what he could do. I hated it, but I got the message.

Halfway through the suspension I was sitting in my office writing out cheques of doubtful authenticity when Barbara Winslow walked in. I looked at her and so far forgot my manners that I didn't even ask her to sit down. She looked ghastly, pale and thin; her fashionable suit hung on her like an op-shop rag.

'I'm sorry,' she said.

'For what?'

'I know that Ian has been giving you a bad time.'

I shrugged. 'He's a murderer. It could be worse.'

She shuddered and dropped into the chair. 'He promised he would stop seeing her. He said he could get clear of all that . . . mess. He hasn't done . . . anything.'

I put a cheque in an envelope and didn't speak. I

searched the desk for a stamp and didn't find one.

'A murderer,' she said.

I nodded.

'Are you sure?'

'Yes.' I looked out the window. The sky was dark and threatening; by the time we got there it'd be raining for sure. I stood. 'Come on, I'll show you.'

On the way I filled her in on the Winslow-da Silva connection and what had happened the night she'd told me I had a wrong number. I took her to the building site on the edge of the Darling Harbour development. The rain started to slant down and the light dimmed. We stood where Luis and I had stood a few weeks back and I pointed things out to her. 'See the crane there? You get the body, in this case it was a Filipino girl named Lela. She'd have been, oh, maybe twenty, and you attach it to this mechanism at the end of the crane. You can release it from the cabin.' I traversed the muddy landscape with my finger. 'See the dark smudges, beyond those mullock heaps? They're holes for foundations and underground installations. They go down a long way. Lot of water in them now. You can't approach them on foot; it's all honeycombed under there, not reinforced yet. Are you following me?'

Her face was wet with rain and tears. 'Yes,' she said.

'Okay. You swing the crane out over the hole and you drop the body. You have to be good at it but the men who do it get some practice, courtesy of animals like your husband. Eventually a million tons of concrete and steel complete the job.'

We walked away, both coatless and hatless and soaked to the skin. I hailed a taxi and Barbara Winslow got into it, moving like a shocked accident victim. Abruptly, she wound the window down.

'I can divorce him,' she said fiercely, 'and pull the political plug on him.'

'Do it,' I said. 'Please.'

A month later the Winslow divorce was in the papers. A little after that, Winslow was sacked from Cabinet for misleading the Parliament. An election was coming up and one of the party bright boys, a favourite of the Premier's, was nominated for pre-selection in Winslow's seat. The rain had stopped and the patches of mould that had begun to sprout and spread on my walls retreated and dried out. My suspension period expired and I went back to work.

High Integrity

GEORGE Marr was the Credit Comptroller at Partner Bros which, if it wasn't the biggest department store chain in Sydney, was rapidly getting that way. To me, he looked absurdly young for his job, but that might have been because I was feeling a fraction too old for mine. He was a slightly built, fair character with a fresh complexion. His hair was cut short and I suspected that he put something on it to keep it as neat as it was. His white shirt was as crisp and fresh as if he'd just put it on a few minutes before, although it was 11 am.

'Mr Hardy,' Marr said, 'have you got a Partner Card?'

'No. I've got a Medicare card and MasterCard. I was hoping to limit my card-holding to them.'

Marr raised one fair eyebrow and looked younger still. 'You don't approve of cards?'

'These days I might have a couple I don't even know about, the way things are going.'

'Cards are the future.'

'They're all right for poker.'

He digested that while I looked around his office. It was neat, stocked with everything he'd need. His secretary was holding his calls and the boldly written entry in the appointments diary open on the desk in front of him showed that I had twenty minutes.

'Well,' he said, 'I suppose that attitude will help keep you objective.'

'What *is* the objective, Mr Marr?'

His expression showed that he didn't like jokes

that early in the day; perhaps he didn't like them at all. 'The Partner Card enables you to credit shop in any of our stores with a minimum of fuss. The system is completely computerised—high integrity, the most sophisticated data base and . . . '

'Hold it. You've lost me.'

'It doesn't matter. There are more than 20,000 card-holders, state-wide.'

'That's more than members of the Liberal Party. It sounds wonderful for your . . . merchandising. What's the problem?'

'The card is being forged. The system is being used fraudulently.'

'Ah.' I sat back in the comfortable seat and thought about what I'd seen on the way to Marr's office. I'd passed several million dollars worth of electronic junk on the way to a lift which had flashed by three floors crammed with 'Home', 'Fashion', 'Style' and 'Recreational' junk. Partners was organised in 'Lifestyle Themes'; you set out to buy a box of matches and you ended up with a barbecue.

'It's serious,' Marr said. 'We've lost close to a hundred thousand dollars at last count.'

'When did you notice it?'

'At a credit audit a week ago. It was plain to see. The stock balance and credit account ratios . . . but I wouldn't expect you to understand the technical details.'

'You'd be right. We private detectives don't understand much. The whole of life is a voyage of discovery for us.'

'Are you trying to be funny, Mr Hardy? I was told you were capable and close-mouthed, not that you were a humorist.'

'I'm not trying hard. Give me the details you think I'll understand, Mr Marr, and I'll try to help you.'

I'm computer-illiterate, but Marr filled me in as

best he could. The phony cards had been used mostly in the electronic sub-section of 'Home' but also in some luxury 'Fashion' sections and in 'Out-of-doors' which had lost a prefabricated garage. A lot of liquor had been liberated too but I couldn't work out whether it came from 'Style' or 'Recreation'.

I scribbled notes while Marr talked. When he stopped I tried to show how sharp I was. 'I can see how they could walk out with the booze and the VCRs, but not a garage.'

'No, that was odd.' He consulted a file on his desk. 'The garage was delivered to an address where the home owner had no knowledge of it. The home owner didn't even shop in Partners.' Marr said this as if it was a matter for deep regret.

'I'll need that address,' I said. 'Also all the names and addresses on the phony cards and details on the people who could have helped from the inside. You know it has to be something like that, don't you?'

He sighed, 'Unhappily, yes. It's a terrible thing —Partners has the best employee record in the industry, bar none. Well, I've anticipated you.' He slid a sheet of paper across the desk. About a dozen names were listed along with addresses and jobs— Electronics Manager; Credit 2IC; Sales & Stock (Liquor); Accounts etc. The names were in two columns, one headed hardware, the other software. I tapped the headings. 'What's this?'

Marr's smile made him look schoolboyish. 'Our little joke—the "hardware" is the selling staff, who interface with the customers; the "software" is the computing staff, who . . . '

'Don't say it. All right, this is the address of the home owner, is it? And let me guess, this is your private phone number at the top. You've got an efficient secretary, Mr Marr.'

'Top computing facilities.'

'Yeah, well that could be your problem. In the old days you just looked and waited until you could slam the till on the hand in it.'

'Times have changed. At first we hoped it was just someone manipulating the programs, but it became clear that false cards were involved. That made it a hands-on situation. That's why you're here.'

I couldn't have taken any more of that kind of language but my time was up anyway. Marr handed me over to Kelvin Lean, the internal security officer, who grudgingly took me on a tour so I could get a sly look at the 'hardware'. After that I went to the Personnel section where Lean showed me photographs of the others.

'This is a smooth operation,' he said. 'I'll be blunt, Hardy. I can't see why I can't handle it myself.'

I didn't say anything. What Lean didn't know was that his name appeared on my list and it was entered under both headings.

My strategy was pretty simple—investigate the people on the list looking for changes in the patterns of their lives. Few people who suddenly come into money can resist displaying it, particularly when the money has been acquired dishonestly. And criminal association is not just limited to inarticulate phone calls between nicknames; it involves time and travel, changes in routines and rendezvous. It makes sense—if you suddenly came into a fortune would you keep on buying your fish fingers at Franklins? The hell you would.

Just to get started, I picked on Morris Guest, the fat, florid manager of the electronics section, as a subject. I followed him out of the store on his lunch hour. He went along George Street and took the underpass to the Queen Victoria Building. It was early February; the kids had just gone back to school and it was a little too early for the shops to be pushing Easter. A quiet time. Guest took the escalator to the top floor. From the close inspection he gave everything—the fancy paving, the polished brass, the stained glass—you'd have thought it was his money they'd used to fix it up.

On the Albert Walk he stood opposite a shop that sold imported rugs and wall hangings. He nodded with approval as customers entered and exited; then he went to the coffee shop and took a seat. I watched from fifty metres away. A large woman, almost as high-coloured as Guest himself, came from the shop. She joined Guest in the eatery; he rose from his chair and pecked her cheek the way a husband does when he's hit the same spot five thousand times before. I left when they started on their lunch—double serves of frankfurts and sauerkraut, iced chocolates with whipped cream and a bushel of bread rolls. I'd check Morris Guest out a little further in Epping where he lived, but my tentative assessment was that he was too soft and comfortable to steal.

Over the next few days I plied my trade. I followed people home and watched them at night. I picked them up in the morning and went to work and lunch with them. I went to laundromats and the movies, McDonald's and wine bars. I walked a lot, stood around a lot and didn't get much sleep. After a week and a bit I'd eliminated all but three of the suspects for various reasons—some too timid, others too family-oriented, some too lazy, some too sporting and so on. The weekend was tough: I watched Kent Hayward ('Software') play golf at Royal Eastern; Colin McKemmish ('Hardware') went to the races and the dogs but didn't bet much; Daphne Lewis went straight from her accounts department job at Partners into her role as freelance caterer. She worked non-stop through the weekend and looked more tired on Monday morning than she had on Friday night.

The garage had been delivered to an elderly widow who lived in a flat in Bondi, three floors up. She found it very funny.

'Why didn't they send me something useful?' she said. 'Like a waterbed? Tell 'em I wanna waterbed next time.'

The break came when I was talking with Kelvin Lean in the Partners canteen the following week. Lean I'd eliminated early in the piece. He was obsessed with *machismo* and self-improvement—went horse-riding, pistol-shooting, took karate lessons, read Ayn Rand. If he'd caught himself being dishonest he'd have handcuffed himself and called the cops. Lean seemed better disposed towards me because I wasn't making progress. I remarked that Kent Hayward seemed like an indoor type—he was tall and thin with a manner something like an art gallery director, part aesthete, part party-goer—and wasn't much of a golfer despite the expensive equipment and membership of a club where the fees were steep.

'Golf?' Lean said. 'That's new for Hayward.'

'How do you know?'

Lean fidgeted and made a train with the sugar cubes. I stared at him with my I've-got-my-teeth-in-your-ankle-and-I'm-not-letting-go look.

'Staff file,' he mumbled.

'I saw them. They had work experience, references, financial stuff. That's all.'

'Private/Staff.'

'Jesus! Look, Kelvin, I was supposed to have access to everything. Do I have to talk to Marr again about this?'

'I don't even know what *this* is. That's my gripe.'

'Okay. Maybe you'll be flattered. Marr kept you in the dark because you were a suspect.' I explained

114

the way of it to him while he turned his sugar cube train into Stonehenge. When I finished he cracked his knuckles.

'Maybe I can help.'

'You can help by showing me these private files.'

'Right.'

We went to his office and Lean transformed himself from 'hardware' to 'software' by switching on his desk computer and dancing his fingers over the keyboard. In a couple of seconds Kent Hayward's private life was on screen. There was a lot of it. Hayward was divorced and paying maintenance and child support for three. According to the file he had no sporting interests.

'Look at this,' Lean said. 'He goes on a pricy holiday last September. First time ever.'

Hayward had used the firm's holiday service to book himself into the Tropicana Hotel at Surfers Paradise for six days. The holiday had upped his indebtedness to Partners Holiday Club but he seemed to be coping with the extra monthly instalments. 'Could be,' I said. 'But people change. Take stock of themselves. Slow down.'

'Come into money?'

'Win it on the horses.'

Lean smiled and the grooves in his over-trained, gaunt face deepened into ruts. 'This is it. I can smell it.'

I had to think quickly. The last thing I needed was Lean sneaking around cracking his knuckles and smelling things. I must have looked doubtful because he held up one hand placatingly while he punched keys with the other. 'Don't worry. I won't interfere. I just wanted to be asked. You might give me a favourable citation in your report if it works out.'

If you can't beat them, join them. 'You've got it,' I said.

The 'Private/Staff' files revealed nothing of interest about the other suspects and Hayward firmed as favourite. It was a bit like shooting with a telescopic sight; when the lines intersected you were in focus and on target. I went home and caught up on some sleep which was easy to do because I was living alone, apart from a cat, and visitors were rare and getting rarer. I told myself that I was lying fallow socially and sexually, rejuvenating. I told this to the cat too, but the cat didn't believe it any more than I did.

My first move was to check on Hayward's golf partners. My lawyer of many years standing and suffering, Cy Sackville, was a member at Royal Eastern. I called him and began by asking what his handicap was.

'Scruples,' he said. 'When did you start playing straight man, Cliff?'

'I'm working on it. What kind of people do you play golf with at Royal Eastern?'

'Oh, judges, lawyers, doctors, stockbrokers, embezzlers, all kinds, why?'

'I'd like to find out who a member by the name of Kent Hayward played with last weekend. Could you get the names?'

'Nothing easier. From the book. You want the scores?'

'No, thanks. When?'

Cy supposed he could fit in nine holes the following morning to relax him for his afternoon in court. He proposed a drink in the club bar at noon.

By then I'd had too much sleep and too much of my own company. I was refreshed, showered and shampooed and taking an interest in every woman I saw between seventeen and seventy. The waitress in the Royal Eastern bar was about thirty and moderately good looking. When she served me my

116

Swan Light my blood raced. Sackville wandered in and ordered Perrier.

'How'd you do?' I said.

'Forty-one, double bogeyed the eighth, bugger it. Here's what you want.'

He handed me a slip of paper. The bar was almost empty but I kept my voice low. 'Clyde Teasdale, Reginald Broderick, Montague Porter. That wouldn't be Monty Porter, would it?'

Sackville sipped Perrier. 'Believe so. Any help?'

'Could be. Thanks a lot. What's the case this afternoon?'

He yawned. 'One of the doctors claims one of the lawyers was embezzling from him.'

'Was he?'

'Probably, but we'll sort it out.'

Monty Porter, if he wasn't actually Mr Big, was Mr Big Enough. If he'd been responsible for half the things that were alleged against him he'd never have had time to wash his socks. Gambling, pimping and drugs were his mainstays, but he probably financed some heavier stuff as well. Monty was married to Marjorie Legge who had a high profile in the fashion industry and the right-wing media, so for every allegation against him there was a champagne glass raised as well.

A trip to Surfers would have been welcome but I couldn't justify it. I phoned Roger Wallace who operates several detective agencies in the eastern states. When he reached fifty, he picked his Southport agency as the one that most needed his personal touch. I asked him to run a check on the guests in the Tropicana over the period of Hayward's stay. We exchanged pleasantries, agreed on terms and he phoned back towards evening.

'Subject didn't get much of the sun,' Roger said.

117

'Seems he spent most of his time in smoky rooms.'

'Who with?'

'Hard to say, but it could easily have been Monty Porter.'

'Oh?'

'Yeah. Monty was in the Honeymoon Suite at the Tropicana for some of the time. I'll send you a list of the other names if you like.'

'Don't bother. Thanks, Roger.'

'Not working for Marjorie Legge, are you?'

'No, why?'

'Monty was honeymooning without her.'

That was intriguing, but I was more interested in the clear focus I was getting on Kent Hayward. I enlisted Lean's help and took a closer look at Hayward professionally and personally. He was manager in the section of the computer operation that despatched and made up accounts and upgraded the data base as required.

'Box seat,' Lean said.

'What about for forging the cards?'

'That too. He'd know the codes, the cut-outs, everything. Of course, he'd have to know some physics and electronics to make much of it.'

'He does,' I said. 'I've followed him to the library and into bookshops. He'd rather read electronics textbooks than Wilbur Smith.'

'I'm a Ludlum man myself,' Lean said. 'So what next? You going to collar him?'

'There's no direct proof. If he's been careful all the way through he could show up clean.'

'Yeah. I've been doing a little quiet snooping myself. Don't worry, not on the ground. Through the computer—there's something a bit funny about this fraud.'

'Struck me they could've got away with a hell of a lot more if they'd wanted to,' I said.

'There's that. But it looks as if all kinds of things have been tried out, all parts of the program.'

'Don't follow.'

'Goods sent to addresses, goods returned and exchanged, items queried, lots of checking of the data base. You'd have thought they'd run the phony cards through the easiest channels but it hasn't been like that at all. They've gone the tough route most times.'

'As if they were checking that it all worked?'

'That's what it looks like. What d'you make of it?'

'All I can think of is that something bigger is on the way. Thanks Kelvin, you've been a big help.'

'As I say, put it in the report.'

They were the last words I ever heard from Kelvin Lean. A little later, after I'd done some more surveillance of Hayward without result, Marr telephoned to tell me that Lean had killed himself.

'It was a great shock. He was a good man, or so we thought.'

'Me too. Why?'

'He left a note to say that he was afraid he had AIDS.'

'Looked pretty healthy to me.'

'Well, there it is. I suppose the autopsy will tell the story.'

'How did he die?'

'He used his shotgun. I believe. Now, d'you think this could have any bearing on your investigation?'

'Don't know. Do you?'

'No fraudulent card use has been reported in the past week. What have you turned up so far?'

'A suspect with no proof.'

'Any connection with Lean?'

'I'll look into it.'

'If there are no further losses . . . '

'Sure, you'll consider the case closed. Give me a few more days, Mr Marr.'

I didn't believe Kelvin Lean had AIDS or thought he had it. And I didn't believe he committed suicide. I phoned Detective Inspector Frank Parker of the Homicide branch and found the police weren't too convinced either.

'Difficult to say, Cliff. Typed note. Prints on the shotgun but you know . . .'

'What do you think of the AIDS theory?'

'Not gay, no drugs and what was left of him would put you and me to shame for muscle tone. What's your interest?'

'Can't say. When will you get the autopsy report?'

'I can't say. Perhaps when you decide to co-operate.'

Logic led to Hayward. As a working theory: Hayward finds out that Lean has been checking on him through the computer. Hayward has a lot to hide and nasty friends like Monty Porter. Exit Lean. Confronting Hayward seemed like my only option if Partners were going to pull the plug on me. Besides, killing Lean looked like an overreaction to a fraud investigation, even a major one. Maybe I could panic Hayward.

He lived in Woollahra, in a big white building that looked as if it had once been a squatter's townhouse but was now four elegant flats. Elegant but old, or perhaps elegant because old. At 6 pm I was parked on the other side of the road watching the expensive cars swirl around the streets, slip into the garages slotted in under the high-sitting houses or jostle for parking space under the plane trees. Hayward had a garage for his Holden Calais. When he closed the roller door I was only a few metres away. When he put the key in the front door to the building I was by his side.

'Let's go inside, Mr Hayward. Let's talk.'

'Who the hell are you?' He threw back his head, to toss long hair out of his eyes and to look through the bottom part of his bifocal lenses. He had his suit coat over his arm, neatly folded, and he was wearing a bow tie. This made me happier about heavying him. I gripped his elbow and bustled him through the door. He tried to prop but he had no experience in the physical side of life. I kept him moving up the stairs and to the door of his flat by keeping him off balance and increasing the pressure on his arm. He was saying things like 'This is intolerable' but I wasn't listening.

So we were in the passageway of his flat and I was doing fine when suddenly things went wrong. First, a man appeared out of nowhere; he moved smoothly, seeming to take all the time in the world, and he shot Hayward between the eyes. I felt Hayward sag away from me and collapse. I flattened myself against the wall and tried to reach for my .38 knowing all the time that I'd be much, much too slow.

The gunman knew it too; he sighted on my chest and gestured for me to drop my hand. I did it; at that range he couldn't miss.

'Well,' he said, 'what's this?'

Another man edged cautiously from a room off the passage. The gunman was medium-sized and wide with a bald head and an almost immobile face. The second man was younger, not out of his twenties. He had long dark hair and a slack, shocked expression on his face. He said, 'Shoot him,' so I liked him less than the other who could've shot me but hadn't tried.

'This isn't the bargain basement, sport. I don't do it in job lots.'

'Come on,' the dark one said. 'He seen everythink. You've gotta . . . '

121

'I don't have to do anything. Look at him. The man's carrying a gun. He could be a cop. Or he could be someone I can talk to.'

'That's right,' I croaked.

'Shit! You just want more money.'

The gunman kept his pistol, which looked like a silenced .22, very steady. 'That'd help,' he said. 'Let's get out of the hall. We can sit down and you can use the phone.'

We went through to the big living room which was dark because all the curtains had been drawn against the light and the heat. The gunman didn't seem to have any trouble seeing; he gestured for me to sit in a chair in the corner and for the other man to use the phone.

'Hey, don't give me orders. Just kill him.'

'You don't have the clout to order a kill, friend.'

The dark man picked up the phone and hit the buttons. He waited, began to speak and stopped. 'Okay,' he said. 'Ten minutes, but tell him it's important.' He read the phone number slowly and clearly and hung up. 'We gotta wait.'

The gunman smiled; until then his face had been so still I was surprised he could do it. 'Why don't you make us a drink, Charley?' he said.

'Fuck you. And my name isn't Charley, it's ... '

'Shut up, you bloody amateur. Charley'll do. Get us a drink, unless you'd rather hold the gun?'

My eyes had grown used to the gloom; it was a big room with a bay window and some low, unobtrusive furniture. The hi-fi looked good and new, so did the TV and VCR. The gunman sat three metres from me and out of the way of all distraction. He saw me judging distance and angles and shook his head. Charley came in with two drinks, whisky and ice.

'One for him, too.'

'What the fuck for?'

'You're paining me, you know that? I didn't like

122

having to bring you along in the first place and I'm liking it less. Just do as I say. It might help him talk. By the way, sport. You might put the gun on the table here. Easy.'

I took out the .38 and put it on the coffee table. I had to lean almost out of my chair to reach it. The gunman would have had to get up to take it but he didn't bother. He gestured for me to sit back. Charley returned with a solid Scotch and I took a drink thinking that the odds had shrunk from short to hopeless.

'Name?'

'Hardy.'

'Cop?'

I shook my head. 'Private. Partners hired me to look into the card business.'

He nodded. 'Anything to trade?'

I shook my head again. I was thinking about throwing the glass and risking a .22 in the body, but the precise way Hayward had been plugged deterred me.

'This is a big operation,' Charley said. 'The trump won't want any loose ends.'

I jerked my thumb at the passage. 'Is that what he was?'

'Yeah. He was leavin' tracks.'

I drank some more Scotch and sneered at him.

'Big operation my arse,' I said. 'Hitting a department store for a few thousand. Fake credit cards. That's not big, it's medium at best. I think our friend here better worry about getting his fee.'

'He'll get it,' Charley said. 'This is really big. Three dead men.'

'I make it two, Lean and Hayward.'

'I was countin' you, arsehole.'

'You talk too much,' the gunman said contemptuously. He sipped his drink. 'Why don't you just tell him all you know while you're at it?'

Charley threw his Scotch straight down. 'Why not? He's dead when the phone rings. You think the Partners stuff is small time? You're right. But it's a practice, you dumb arsehole, and it's not the only one.'

Suddenly it all made sense—the thorough testing of the data base, the relatively small yield. 'Practice for what?'

'I wouldn't,' the gunman said. 'I don't want to know.'

'Screw you. For when they bring in the Australia Card. We're gonna be ready to crack it wide open. We'll get millions out of it before they know what's fuckin' happened to them.' He smiled triumphantly but his face still looked unambitious and dumb.

'Who's we?' I said.

The phone rang. I finished my drink and looked at the gunman who put down his glass and indicated that I should do the same.

'Yeah,' Charley said into the phone. 'He's here.' He listened and then extended the phone to the gunman. 'Wants to talk to you.'

The gunman got up in an easy fluid movement, kept the pistol on me and took the receiver. He listened, said 'Understood,' and handed the receiver to Charley.

'What'd he say?'

'He said to make it a double. Sorry.' He shot Charley in the head. I moved like a twelve-year-old, springing from the chair, hitting the floor in a diving roll and grabbing my .38 from the table all at once. I heard the .22 crack and I got one shot off that went into the ceiling, but by then I was almost behind a high-backed chair and the gunman was facing a heavier calibre gun and a more desperate man. He fired once at the chair but he was already on the retreat. He was quicker than me; by the time I was clear of the chair and had hurdled Charley's body, the passage was empty apart from the slumped body of Kent Hayward. The door was flapping open. A face appeared in the opening, a woman.

'Hey,' she yelled.

I said, 'Call the police.' Then I looked at Hayward and the gun in my hand. I tried to look reassuring but she covered her face with her hands and shrank back. 'No, don't bother,' I said. 'I'll do it myself.'

The bodies brought Frank Parker, who listened quietly to what I had to say while a forensic man bustled around the room and the uniformed cops dealt with the ambulance, the other residents in the flats and sundry spectators. I gave Frank everything, including Monty Porter's name and his connection with Hayward. I told him what Charley had said about the practice run for the Australia Card, as close to word for word as I could recall it.

'They're starting early,' was all he said.

'Think you'll be able to tie Porter in with this guy?' I pointed to the chalk on the chair which marked where Charley had died.

'What d'you reckon? Describe the killer for me.'

'Thirty, maybe a bit more; bald head, maybe shaved; brown eyes, maybe contacts; five nine . . . '

'But maybe he had lifts in his shoes. Maybe his teeth were false. No, nothing'll tie up to anything else. Well, your clients'll be happy. You've given them Hayward. End of story.'

'You might find out he owed Porter money.'

Frank laughed. 'Porter hasn't got any money. Not a cent. How he lives in a two million dollar house when he's so poor beats me.'

'Will you tell the Federal people about this?'

'I'll tell them. It'll take me a couple of days to write the reports. Then you know what'll happen? They'll issue a statement confirming the high integrity of the Australia Card.'

I shrugged. 'Who cares?'

Frank looked at me. 'Not very public-spirited.'

I watched the forensic guy put my .38 in a plastic bag and label it. I thought about the statements I was going to have to make and the forms I'd have to fill in to get it back. Bureaucracy. 'I don't want a bloody Australia Card,' I said. 'When I want another card I ask the dealer.'

'Box on!'

I'M finished with boxing,' I said. 'I don't go and I don't watch it on TV.'

'Why not?' Jack Spargo drew a stick figure in the dust on my office window. He gave the figure boxing gloves.

'I read about a British medical report on the brain damage boxers suffer. One fight can do it, an amateur fight even. A bloody spar can kill a few thousand brain cells.'

'Bullshit.'

'I had a few amateur fights myself, Jack. D'you realise that I might be suffering brain damage?' I looked around the office, at the walls that needed painting, the carpet that needed replacing. 'I could be smarter than this maybe.'

Spargo spun around from the window and laughed. He still moved well although he was pushing sixty. 'That's for sure. Well, I'm sorry that you won't help a mate.'

'He's your mate, not mine.'

'Cliff.'

'He's a has-been. A never-was.'

'He went ten rounds with Foreman.'

'Foreman's a preacher of some kind now, isn't he? He must've got religion earlier than we thought to have let Roy Belfast last ten rounds.'

Spargo looked hurt. He opened his Gladstone bag and put a battered clippings book on my desk. I didn't want to look at it. 'I'm a private detective, Jack, not a nursemaid. Do you realise how silly it'd look? "Ex-champ hires minder".'

'The Yanks've done it for years.'

'They elect senile presidents and cut up all their food like babies before they eat it too. Doesn't mean we have to do the same.'

Spargo pushed the book towards me. 'He's a good bloke.'

I opened the book. Just the way it was put together made me sad. These days, sports stars and actors keep their cuttings in fancy books with plastic envelope leaves; Roy Belfast's history was in a thick school exercise book—the clippings were pasted in lumpily; some were folded. They were already yellow and dry like fallen leaves. It was a familiar story with a few variations. Roy Belfast was a country boy, big, with a straight eye and a fairly fast left jab. He won the Australian heavyweight championship at nineteen from nobody in particular. There was no one much around for him to fight and he was ready to go stale when he got a chance to meet a Jamaican for the Commonwealth title. Roy was outclassed for five rounds but then he got lucky and cut the Jamaican who had to retire. Then the Jamaican went to jail on a drugs charge and Roy defended the title against a Brit cast in the same mould as 'Phainting' Phil Scott.

Give him his due, Spargo handled Belfast well. He avoided the serious Americans and got him a few fights with people he could handle low on the card of big fights. Then the chance to fight Foreman came up. I turned over the pages slowly.

'I shouldn't have done it,' Spargo said.

'No, probably not.'

Foreman was regrouping after his loss to Ali. It had been a big paynight for Roy, bigger than he had any right to expect. Sheer courage kept him upright for ten rounds; I looked at the post-fight photo—Belfast's head was swollen to twice its size and his boyish features were obliterated.

'What happened to all the money?' I said.

128

Spargo shrugged. 'They'd shrunk it down pretty far before it got to us.'

'And now Belfast wants to make a comeback. What does he want to do? Buy a pub and drink himself to a title?'

Spargo shook his head. 'Roy don't drink. Never did. He's been to business college, Cliff. He's studied up on things. Wants capital to open a video store specialising in sports films. He reckons he can make it pay and I want to help him.'

'That's original at least. But it's been twelve years. Belfast must be . . . '

'Eleven years. Roy's thirty-one. That isn't old. Look at Jimmy Connors.'

'Nobody ever beat Jimmy Connors over the head with a tennis racquet. Roy'll get hurt.'

'I don't think so. Three fights and that's all. He's very quick. He'll stay out of trouble.'

'The crowd'll love that,' I said. 'They really appreciate the finer points since Fenech.'

'Fenech's a . . . ' Spargo stopped and grinned. Scar tissue puckered around his eyes and he sniffed through his old fighter's nose. 'You always like a joke, Cliff. Maybe that's why Roy wants you around.'

'I can't see it.'

'You know the creeps that come outa the drains in this business. The proposition merchants, the blokes with a girl who'd like to meet the champ, the pushers?'

'Yeah, I know them.'

'So you can spot them and run interference. Also you know some press people. That'd be useful. Two weeks. Cliff. That's all.'

'Two weeks! That's not long enough to train. Who's he fighting—Boy George?'

'He's been in training three months. This was set up a good while ago. It'll look like a quickie but it ain't.'

'Who, Jack?'

'Boss Tikopia.'

It could have been worse. Tikopia was a Maori who'd beaten all the light heavyweights south of the equator which wasn't saying much. 'What's in it for him? Fighting a has-been?'

'He's built up, like Spinks. Wants to move up and take on the big boys. He figures he can find out what it's like with Roy.'

'What it *was* like.'

'Roy's sharp, Cliff. Weighs 14.1. That's lighter than he usta be.'

I considered it. I weighed 12.2 which was heavier than I usta be. I could do with a couple of weeks boxing training. It was April and a clear, crisp day outside. 'Where's he training?'

'Pearl Beach. Gym up there, big flat an' all. You can move in today.'

Pearl Beach sounded good and I had nothing serious on hand. 'I'll come up and take a look at him. If he looks as if he can stay on his feet for ten rounds I'm in.'

'He's the best heavyweight we've had since . . .'

I held up my hand. 'Don't, Jack. Please don't. Nobody's the best since anybody. That's all bullshit.'

Jack said a name but he said it under his breath. He told me the fight was being promoted by Col Marriott who used to be a lot of things and still was a few besides a fight promoter, not all of them virgin white. But he had the Entertainment Centre booked and a TV deal and Jack said Belfast's expenses were generous so they'd be able to cover my fees. I noticed that there were a few blank pages at the back of the clippings book as I handed it back to Spargo. We shook hands. The next day I packed a bag and drove to Pearl Beach.

I'd seen Belfast fight a few times and knew him slightly. I'd never heard anything against him other than the usual fight talk—pity he wasn't five centimetres taller, or five kilos heavier, or had a bigger punch. Meeting him again, ten or more years later, I was impressed. He was one of those people who seem to improve with age. He hadn't filled out around the middle like most retired fighters, perhaps he was a bit heavier in the shoulders. He'd kept his thick brown hair; his good-natured face carried a few more lines but no noticeable boxing scars.

'Good to see you again, Cliff.'

We shook. 'Hello, Roy. Nice spot you've got here.'

We were standing outside a big house set back a few streets from the beach. Belfast and Spargo had been sitting on deck chairs on the front verandah and had come down the path towards the gate. Spargo looked a bit embarrassed. 'Yeah, well, we've got the back bit.'

Nothing could detract from the good weather and the pleasure of the beach, but Roy Belfast's training camp didn't inspire confidence. The 'gym' was an old hall temporarily fitted out with boxing equipment that had seen better days. The 'flat' was the back half of the big house, a series of lean-tos with small windows and an outside dunny. Against that, morale was high and there were lots of places for Belfast to run and train out of doors.

Roy and Jack Spargo shared a bedroom, I had another room and Rhys Dixon, the sparring partner, slept on a couch in the sitting room. The place was cramped but friendly. We did the usual things— watched TV, played cards and talked boxing. I spent a bit of time on the phone talking to journalists and arranging interviews and photograph sessions. I intercepted some phone calls and pamphlets from an anti-boxing and blood sports group. It wasn't anything a fifty-kilo eighteen-year-old from the Receptionist Centre couldn't have done.

Belfast was sharp in training. He was a tiger for roadwork and delighted in making Jack puff as he tried to keep up on his old hub-geared bike. Sometimes Belfast ran ten or twelve kilometres; I'd run the first three and wait for him and run back. Spargo showed a few videos of Tikopia's fights; if I'd had to fight him I would probably have run the whole twelve kilometres.

Belfast was calm and good-natured most of the time. He put a lot into his sparring sessions with Dixon though, and I thought about that British medical report when I saw Rhys go down after a heavy right, headgear and all. Belfast apologised and helped him up.

'Sorry, Rhys.'

'For what? I slipped.'

One of Spargo's training innovations was beach sparring. He made Belfast wear heavy boots while Rhys jumped around him barefoot. The sand got cut up and Roy had to labour to move his feet and keep his balance. I took a turn at it; Belfast went easy with me but I could sense the strength in his legs and the weight he could have put into his punches with those heavy shoulders. After ten minutes I collapsed, winded.

Belfast grinned. 'You lose if you go down without being hit, Cliff.'

'I'm buggered.'

'Too much wine and sitting about.'

'Wait till you're forty plus, sport.'

'When I'm forty I'll have a string of video shops and be sitting pretty.'

'I hope so, Roy,' I said.

Spargo and Dixon were walking back along the beach towards the car. Belfast pulled off his T-shirt and boots. 'Come for a swim,' he said. 'Give me a chance to have a word with you without Jack around.'

We hit the water together and swam out a hundred metres. Belfast had a hard, chopping stroke, not stylish, but effective. We floated in calm water out beyond the gentle breakers.

'Reckon you're earning your money, Cliff?'

'No.'

'You will.'

'How's that, Roy?'

'Some Enzedders'll be showing up soon. They've got some funny ideas.' He turned his head, took a mouthful of water and expelled it upwards like a whale, except that his body wasn't rounded; it showed flat and hard on the top of the water. I didn't say anything.

'They're coming to check on their investment. When they see the training I'm doing they might want to make certain points.'

'Come on, Roy. I know you've been to college but this is too subtle to make sense.'

He turned over and trod water. He paddled close to me and put his head a few centimetres from mine. 'That's all I want to say. You're working for me and your money comes out of my purse. Right?'

I nodded, as well as you can nod when treading water.

'Everything'll be okay if you just do as I say. When I give the word certain people will be unwelcome. Clear?'

'We'll see,' I said. Belfast swam off, caught a wave and rode it in. It took me three tries to get one—thinking and surfing don't go well together. I wasn't surprised that there was some funny business about the fight. Fights are like horse races —some of them are honest and the trick is to know which ones. But I was still finding Roy Belfast impressive and there was one big point in his favour: no one who intended to throw a fight would train the way he was.

The visitors came the next day, one week before the fight. One was a small, nuggetty guy about

133

jockey-sized, the other was tall, pale and lantern-jawed. Roy and Rhys were working out on the heavy bag when they walked into the gym. Spargo was forcing the stuffing back into a battered medicine ball; I was riding an exercise bike set on EASY. I got off the bike and moved across to block their path towards Spargo.

'Morning, gents.'

'Morning,' the small one said. 'I'm Tim Johnson, here to see Mr Spargo.' He pronounced his name 'Tuhm'—his NZ accent was as thick as pea soup.

'It's all right, Cliff, it's in the contract,' Spargo said. 'Both camps can send a representative to a training session.'

'Right,' Johnson said.

'I'm Cliff Hardy. Would have been polite to phone,' I grumbled.

Johnson ignored that. 'This is Lofty Sargent.' He nodded at his big mate. Lofty nodded too which brought his chin down about level with my head. 'Well, how's the boy?' Johnson glanced across at Roy and Rhys. ''Cept he's no boy, is he? Thirty-three?'

'Thirty-one,' Spargo said, 'younger'n Ali when he beat Foreman. He's in top shape. See for y'self.'

Johnson lit a cigarette and sauntered across towards the heavy bag. He watched Roy throw a few punches and puffed on his smoke. Belfast put a short right into the bag, spun on his heel and plucked the cigarette from Johnson's mouth.

'Not here, mate, if you don't mind.' He stepped on the butt and threw another punch. Johnson didn't like it but he didn't say anything. He and Lofty watched Roy and Rhys spar for three rounds; his hands moved towards his cigarettes a few times but he checked the movement. Roy gave it everything he had and Rhys just managed to stay on his feet. Spargo was surprised; I was surprised and Rhys was surprised, but that was nothing to Johnson's reaction. He winced as Roy's punches landed and muttered under his breath. I worked the corner and after the second round Roy spoke around his mouth-guard as I sponged him off. 'Johnson'll want to talk to you. All you have to do is act dumb.'

'I feel dumb,' I said. 'What is this? You practically put Rhys through the ropes.'

Spargo was in Rhys' corner. 'How're the hands, Roy?' he barked.

Belfast's voice was louder than it needed to be. 'Like rocks.' He boxed his way 'Gentleman Jim' style through the third and went off to shower.

Spargo winked at Johnson. 'I'll be over to see your bloke tomorrow.'

Johnson didn't reply and Lofty maintained his policy of strict silence. They left. Roy fell into an intense talk on tactics with Spargo and Rhys which left me nothing to do but wander out of the hall into the sunshine. I hadn't gone twenty metres down the quiet street before a car pulled up and Lofty bounded out to stand in front of me. He cast a big shadow. Johnson got out of the car and stood behind me.

'Why don't we go for a little ride, Hardy?' Johnson said. 'Bit of a talk.'

It wasn't a time for heroics; I whipped around and jumped at Johnson. I grabbed his arms, spun him clockwise and pushed them up his back towards his thin, wrinkled neck. He resisted and he was strong for a small man, but I had the weight and the leverage on him. I pressed him back against the car, hard. 'Back off, Lofty,' I said. 'Or I'll break his arms.' I rammed the right arm a few centimetres higher. 'I noticed you were a southpaw, Timmo, so I'll bust this one first, Okay?'

'Easy, Lofty,' Johnson said. 'No need for this, Hardy.'

'Tell Lofty to go for a drive then. He can drive, can't he?'

'It's one of the things he does good. Another one'd be to push your bloody face in.'

'That's what I thought,' I said. 'Send him for cigarettes and we'll talk.'

Johnson jerked his head at Lofty. The giant had been edging closer and I don't know what I'd have done if he'd decided that Johnson's arms didn't matter. He opened the car door; I pulled Johnson away. Lofty's face was expressionless.

'Be on the other side of the street in twenty minutes,' I said.

'I don't like you. You're a smart Aussie shuht.' Lofty had an accent like Johnson's; he got into the driver's seat and spoke through the open window.

'That's a puhty,' I said. 'I was looking forward to us being great mates. Like fuhsh an' chuhps.'

Lofty started the motor and drove off with a squeal of tyres. I eased the pressure on Johnson's arms slowly, watching his feet for any sneaky moves. He rubbed his elbows and massaged his wrists. 'Now I see what your job is,' he said. 'Sorta like mine.'

'I doubt it. You wanted to talk?'

'Is Belfast showing off or what?'

'You're talking, I'm listening.'

'He hasn't got any crazy idea about beating Tikopia, has he?' Johnson flexed his fingers and reached into his coat pocket for his cigarettes. He lit up and blew smoke away from me.

'He's in it to win it as far as I know.'

'That's crazy. He hasn't got a chance.'

'So, what's your problem?'

'I should've said not much of a chance.'

'Maybe you shouldn't say anything. Maybe you should just piss off.'

'Yeah. But you might give Belfast a bit of advice, a message like.' He took a drag on his cigarette and picked his words carefully. 'We want a good fight. Just tell 'um that. We want a good fight.' He turned and walked across the street.

Later, back at the flat, I got a chance to talk to Belfast alone. He was doing something you rarely see a fighter do—reading a book. 'Tim Johnson left you a message,' I said.

'Oh, what's that?'

'Said to tell you they want a good fight.'

'Don't we all.'

'Come on, Roy.' He kept his big, plain face impassive and looked at me. It was a strange moment; a lot of my time is spent in getting people to talk. Sometimes they want to, sometimes they don't. When they don't you have to charm them or intimidate them. I didn't think either technique would work with Roy Belfast. 'Don't bullshit me, Roy. I'm not the White Knight, I'm not going to ask for a Royal Commission. Is it a fix?'

'Keep y'voice down, d'you want Jack to hear? He won't even use the word fix to talk about mending something. D'you really think I'd train like this just to go into the tank?'

I shook my head. Roy punched me on the shoulder; maybe just to be friendly, maybe not. The shape of the bruise might tell me. 'Trust your instincts, Cliff,' he said. 'Ever study accountancy?'

'Christ, no.'

He picked up his texbook and turned a page. 'It's interesting. More interesting than boxing.'

A few days later Spargo announced that he was going to town to watch Tikopia train. Neither Roy nor Rhys was interested but Roy insisted that I accompany Jack.

'What should I watch out for?' I said. 'Propositions or pick handles?'

'Hospitality,' Roy said. 'You noticed there was no grog up here?'

I had noticed, in fact I'd formed the habit of going to the pub for a couple of quiet glasses in the evening. 'I thought that was standard.'

'It's not for my benefit, I never touch it. Keep an eye on Jack; if he starts drinking he's likely to do something foolish. Keep Johnson away from him.'

'How am I going to do that? It's a free country.'

Roy's face became super-serious. 'Have you got a gun?'

'Yes.'

'Take it with you—Johnson might need reminding it's a free country.'

Tikopia was training at Billy Groom's in Chippendale. I drove down with Jack and parked the Falcon outside the gym. I glanced up and down the street in case Lofty was hiding behind a cement truck.

'You look edgy, Cliff,' Spargo said as we got out of the car. 'What's the matter? We're bloody invited.'

I thought about questioning Spargo on a few points of detail about the fight but I decided against it. I realised that I had confidence in Roy Belfast which is an unusual thing to be able to say of a boxer except about the few specific things he can do in the ring. We went up two flights to the gym which was a first class set-up: the equipment was new; the ropes to the ring were white and taut, not the grey sagging things they become when men's sweaty backs have rubbed along them for a while.

Tikopia was in the ring sparring with a light-coloured Aborigine who did nothing aggressive. Spargo stood off and watched for a minute before going over to join three men by the ring. One was Johnson; one was Col Marriott, the promoter; the other I didn't know. Marriott made the introductions; the third man was Reg Warner, Tikopia's trainer. He and Spargo shook hands.

'Should be a good night,' Warner said.

'Good gate, considering we've got the TV.' Marriott looked warily at me and Johnson. We stood by, strong and silent. I wondered where Lofty was.

Tikopia and his sparring partner circled the ring. The Aborigine jabbed, back-pedalled and weaved; Tikopia stalked him, trying to catch him in a corner or against the ropes. He succeeded enough for Warner to nod happily. When he had the range Tikopia got in some head and body punches. Smart stuff. Johnson sidled up beside me. 'Feelin' tough today, Hardy?'

I opened my denim jacket enough to let him see the Smith & Wesson in its holster. 'No, bit fragile as a matter of fact.'

'Give Belfast the message?'

'Yeah. I'm wondering if I should mention it to Warner and Marriott.'

'Mention what? They wouldn't know what you was talkin' about.' He moved away. I sat down next to Spargo who was gazing at the spar intently.

'He's quick,' he said. 'Thirteen and a half stone, d'y'reckon?'

I shrugged. 'Not more. The other bloke's not trying.' Just then Tikopia brushed aside a left lead, moved in close and thumped the Aborigine in the ribs. He grunted and tried to cover up; Tikopia hit him with a right. The Aborigine tried a flurry of punches which Tikopia walked through. He banged in a solid rip to the mid-section which brought his opponent's glove down, then Tikopia let go a sharp left hook which he halted just a centimetre from the unprotected jaw. He gripped the Aborigine's head between his gloves and laughed.

'Had you then, brother,' he said thickly through the mouthguard.

Warner grinned and threw the towel into the ring. Everyone laughed except Jack Spargo.

Spargo, who was never loquacious, was quieter than ever on the drive north. We were near Woy Woy when he snapped his fingers. 'Knew I'd seen that bloke before,' he said. 'He was riding in Sydney in 1980 and got rubbed out for ten years. Don't think his name was Johnson though.'

I grunted and moved out around a semi. 'What's the betting on the fight, Jack?'

'Varies. I got threes.'

'Who on?'

He almost dislocated his neck turning it to look at me. 'What do you mean?'

'What I said.'

'I never bet against one a me own fighters in me life. Well, only once.'

'How was that?'

'Clever bastard, thought he was. I knew he was gonna dive and he didn't know I knew. I did it to teach him a lesson.'

'Did he learn it?'

'No, he didn't. Roy's straight, Cliff. You know that.'

'Yeah. So where does this Johnson fit in?'

'Search me. All I know is, Roy'll be trying like he always has.'

'I'll worry about Johnson then,' I said. 'You can tell Roy what to do about those rips when he's on the ropes.'

Spargo didn't say anything but his face set into lines of concentration like a chess master's.

Roy had three more days to train, then he'd ease up and just keep loose for twenty-four hours before the fight. In the closing days he took care to run on flat surfaces, avoiding the cambered beach or anything else that might injure his ankles; Spargo was specially careful with the hand bandages and the adjustment of the headgear. The caution irritated the risk-taker in Belfast, but the accountant in him saw the necessity.

Rhys Dixon had some acting talent, like a lot of Welshmen, and he could play Tikopia's part in the ring well enough. Spargo worked out a manoeuvre whereby Roy, as soon as he felt the ropes at his back, side-stepped fast away from a left rip, claimed and threw a jolting left into Rhys' unprotected ribs. After a few sessions Dixon's side was sore and bruised. He wore the bruise like a medal. 'That's a sweet move,' he said.

A few reporters showed up, more than I expected. It was a dull time in the sports calendar so interest in the fight was unnaturally high. Roy picked up a few bucks doing a photo ad for a light beer. Spargo fretted at the amount of time he had to spend standing still but Belfast took it with good humour. I intercepted a phone call from Johnson.

'He's in the middle of a couple of hundred push-ups,' I said. 'It's not convenient.'

'You're a smart-arse,' Johnson said. 'I hope he isn't.'

I was being well paid to get a suntan, lose weight, put a double nelson on a jockey and be a smart arse.

Belfast was booked into a motel near Hyde Park. On the drive down I asked him if there was anything special he wanted me to do. He glanced at Spargo who was asleep in the back seat; Roy had slept like a child the night before, Spargo hardly at all.

'You'll be in the corner. Just do everything Jack says then and stick close to me after the finish.' He blinked a few times and rubbed his hand over his gingery three-day growth. 'You talk to Tikopia at all?'

'No. Got a good look at him though.'

'What sort of a bloke is he, d'you reckon?'

I remembered the broad, brown face topped by crinkling hair and the good-natured way he held his opponent's head after he'd pulled the punch that could have torn it off.

'Looked to have a sense of humour.'

Roy smiled and relaxed. 'Good,' he said.

I walked down towards the ring behind Roy Belfast and Jack Spargo. I was wearing jeans and a white T-shirt, sneakers. I carried a towel. Jack carried a bucket in which he had a bottle of distilled water, some condiment for cut eyes, petroleum jelly, a sponge, tape and other tools of the trade. I had my gun under the towel. Roy did some of the obligatory weaving and shadow boxing down the aisle; his back looked huge in the dressing gown; the towel draped around his neck made it look as if a massive head sat directly on massive shoulders.

The house was full and noisily enthusiastic after a better than usual preliminary card. People reached out to shake Roy's hand and shout encouragement. Five metres behind me I could hear the same people saying the same things to Tikopia. A big difference in the atmosphere from the old-time fight nights struck me immediately—no smoke. Smoke used to hang around the ring like a grey mist. All the old-time boxers were involuntary smokers, but when they fought fifteen and twenty rounds with light gloves and no eight count that was the least of their worries. Now we had two doctors in attendance and you couldn't be saved by the bell, but their brain sacks were going to bounce off the walls of their skulls just the same.

Jack got into the ring with Roy after laying out his equipment. All he wanted me to do was hand him things and not knock over the water bottle. Roy and Tikopia bounced and pounded the air, shrugging their shoulders and loosening their necks. The announcer put a little Chicago into his voice as he proclaimed Tikopia 'the champeen of the South Pacific Commonwealth' which was scrambling it a bit. The crowd as a whole cheered loudest for Roy but some Maoris grouped together in a couple of rows at ringside helped to even things up. A two-metre blonde in spike heels and a flesh-coloured body stocking walked around the ring holding up a board with '1' printed on it. I helped her out through the ropes and she kissed me. Roy and Tikopia touched gloves and then Roy hit the spread brown nose with a sharp left and the cheers for sex turned into cheers for blood.

They felt each other out in the early rounds but, like old pros, they managed to put a good bit of work into it—jabs from Roy, rushes from Tikopia and ducking and weaving from both. In the corner Spargo kept up a constant stream of advice: *Don't drop your right, you're dropping your right. Watch his head in close, he's looking to butt you. Keep outa his corner; try 'im downstairs* . . .

The crowd was happy with what it was getting; yells went up when Roy took a hard punch on his gloves or when the referee bullocked the fighters apart and when the blonde walked around in her body stocking. I located Lofty at ringside, behind Tikopia's corner and a few rows back. Johnson sat immediately behind the corner and leaned forward occasionally to talk to one of the Maori's handlers. Warner was like Spargo—transported to that place where only wounds and water and towels and the pummelling of muscles mattered.

By the middle of the fight the pattern was clear; Tikopia was the organiser. He dictated the pace and movement around the ring. To the uninitiated he would have looked a winner, but Roy took many of his punches on his arms and gloves and his counter-punching was effective. He scored cleanly several times and I had it all even going after the seventh which was a good round for Roy.

Johnson was looking worried. He turned around to speak to Lofty and he continued his conversations with the cornerman. The betting fluctuated around me and I had to assume it did the same around Johnson.

In the eighth Belfast took a hard right to the head and sagged. He covered up but he was negative and it was Tikopia's round. In the ninth Tikopia tried a rush, bullocking Roy across to the ropes. As soon as he hit them Roy performed the manoeuvre he'd worked on with Dixon. He performed it perfectly from instinct and with impeccable timing. He side-stepped away from the rip and put all his weight into the punch he landed under Tikopia's armpit. I thought I heard the ribs crack. Roy hit him there again and followed with a straight right that caused Tikopia to drop his hands. The crowd saw the opening and screamed. Roy scored with some classic punches before Tikopia retreated, covering up. He was tough and weathered the round but it was clearly Roy's stanza.

I forgot about the brain sacks and the threatened retinas and roared encouragement to Roy. The blonde was wide-eyed and screaming. She waved her clenched fists and looked as if she wanted to mix it with them in the ring instead of strutting around with her number '10' board.

Most of the crowd watched the last round standing on its feet. Tikopia rushed and swung; Roy back-pedalled and picked him off with jabs. Then Roy stood his ground and slugged. Tikopia landed some good punches in close and Roy retreated. In the last thirty seconds he rallied, moved the Maori around the ring and had him covering up in his, Roy's, corner which always makes a good impression, when the bell sounded.

The ring filled with people; the TV commentator waved his mike and tried to break through the wall of bodies to the fighters. I was hoarse with yelling. I couldn't get into the ring but I worked my way around and was close to Roy's back, with the gun under my towel. I kept my eye on Johnson who stood with Lofty staring up into the crowded ring and rolling an unlit cigarette around in his mouth.

The first judge gave it to Tikopia by two points, the second to Roy by the same margin. The third judge called it a draw and that's what it was. The fighters embraced and the referee held up both right arms. The blonde kissed them both and Spargo and Warner shook hands. Tikopia's wide face was swollen and Roy's upper body was covered with angry red blotches. All bets were off of course and money changed hands only to move back to where it had come from.

Eventually the hugging stopped and the loud buzz of animated conversation died down. Roy left the ring and I stuck close to him and Spargo all the way through the back-slappers and 'champ-sayers' to the dressing room. Spargo chattered excitedly. I lost sight of Johnson and Lofty. Belfast was nervous in the dressing room; he snapped at Spargo as Jack unbandaged his hands and he wouldn't go into the shower.

'Take a look outside, Cliff,' he said. 'See what's happening.'

Before I could move, Marriott breezed in with congratulations and talk of a re-match. Belfast barely spoke to him. When he left I looked out into the corridor. 'Nothing. Getting quieter.'

'Go and get Tikopia. Invite him to a party or somethin'.'

'What is this?' Spargo said.

I went around the slight bend in the passage and knocked at Tikopia's door. Warner stuck his head out.

'Yeah?'

'Roy wants to see your boy.'

I heard the Maori say, 'Tell him I'm comin',' over Warner's protest.

I went back to Roy's room and found Johnson and Lofty there. Johnson's wizened monkey face was screwed up in anger; Lofty was impassive but a look of pleased anticipation showed when he saw me. I thought he was going to crack his knuckles but he didn't. I wasn't too worried, I had the .38 in my back pocket. Then I saw that Johnson was holding a small bottle in his hands. Roy Belfast's eyes were fixed on the bottle.

'You didn't come through,' Johnson said.

'It was a draw,' Belfast said quickly. 'All bets're off. Your people didn't lose anything.'

'Roy?' Spargo's tone was incredulous.

'You don't think a bloody has-been like him could've got this match without arrangements, do you?' Johnson said. 'He was supposed to fold in the seventh. That was a good round for you, the seventh.'

Spargo looked at Roy. 'You did a deal?'

Roy nodded.

Johnson moved closer to him and raised the bottle. Roy was braced, ready to move either way.

'Put it down, Johnson!' I had the gun out and levelled. Johnson's arm tensed and he gave me no choice. I shot him in the right leg. He yelled and the bottle dropped. Belfast dodged. The bottle hit the wall, shattered and sprayed steaming liquid. Spargo yelled as some of it touched his arm. Belfast rushed towards him as he groaned and swore. Lofty growled and came at me with his big arms swinging.

Out of the corner of my eye I saw Johnson reach into his pocket and pull out another bottle. He was lying on the floor only a metre from Roy and Spargo. Lofty lashed at me, caught my shoulder and I dropped the gun. I ducked under the next swing and tried to kick his knee out. I connected with his shin which only slowed him down a fraction. He bullocked me towards the wall and got set to spread me across it when Tikopia appeared in the room. He hammered Lofty in the kidneys. Lofty turned and Tikopia dropped him with a left hook.

Tikopia kept moving; he stepped past Lofty and

gripped Johnson's wrist. The bottle fell from his grasp and Tikopia caught it. Marriott poked his head through the door. 'What's going on?'

'Bad publicity,' Belfast said. 'Keep everyone away.'

The promoter gaped at the two men on the floor and the third, Spargo, nursing his arm and swearing. 'Sounded like a shot.'

'Maori war dance,' I said. 'Plus champagne corks. Go and get a doctor who can keep his mouth shut.'

The door closed. Johnson dragged himself to the wall and whimpered; there was a lot of blood on his leg but it wasn't spraying.

'Shut up!' Tikopia said. He looked down at the unconscious Lofty and nodded approvingly. Spargo pulled himself away from Belfast who was applying a wet towel to his arm. 'Get off,' he said. 'It's all right, burnt meself worse on the stove. What the hell's going on here?'

Tikopia and Belfast looked at each other. The Maori nodded. 'Tikopia's been hooked up with some bad people,' Roy said. 'He wanted to get clear of them. I got the fight by agreeing to throw it but him and me did our own deal.'

Tikopia nodded. He picked up my gun from the floor and handed it to me. 'We thought they'd pull something like this after the fight. Now we've got some evidence and witnesses.'

Tikopia held up the bottle of acid. 'Bad news this,' he said.

'What about the fight?' Spargo said.

Roy dabbed with the wet towel. 'We agreed to a straight fight. If he absolutely had to, Tikopia was going to pay off any losing bets out of his end if I won.'

The Maori grinned. 'Don' have to now.'

'Why?' Spargo said.

'Don't you see it, Jack?' I looked at the fighters

147

—Tikopia's right eye was almost closed but he was grinning, showing big white teeth. Belfast's jaw was swollen from the right he'd copped in the eighth. 'They both wanted to see if they were any good. Tikopia needed to know if he could take a heavyweight's punch and Roy needed to know if he could still do it at all. This game's full of bullshit. They could only trust each other.'

The boxers nodded and touched hands the way they do at the start and end of a fight. 'That's right,' they said.

The Deserter

'I want you to find my son, Mr Hardy,' Ambrose Guyatt said to me. 'He's a soldier.'

An image from *Rambo* flashed before my eyes—gaunt men in rags screaming inside a bamboo cage. I'd watched the movie on a flight from Honolulu to Sydney because I'd finished my book and couldn't sleep. I'm over forty and carry a few un-healed physical and emotional wounds which make me unfit for that kind of action.

'I don't understand,' I said.

'I should say he *was* a soldier. He went absent without leave.'

'For how long?'

'It's not clear. Some weeks.'

'Then he's a deserter.'

Guyatt shifted his well-padded behind on the un-padded chair I have for clients in my office. What's the point in making them too comfortable? They might decide that everything's all right and go away. Guyatt didn't. 'Technically, perhaps. You were in the army yourself, I believe. Malaya. You don't look old enough.'

'It went on longer than people think. If your son's a deserter, Mr Guyatt, the military and the police'll be looking for him. I can't see . . . '

'Julian didn't desert, or if he did he had a good reason. He's not some little guttersnipe; he's edu-cated, he's got background.'

I held the smile in; I've seen backgrounds fade into the far distance and guttersnipes come up with the goods. I got out a fresh note pad and clicked my

149

ballpoint. 'You'd better tell me all about it, Mr Guyatt.'

Like most people feeling their way into a subject, he found it easiest to start with himself. Ambrose Guyatt ran a very profitable business which had blossomed from paper and stationery into printing and copying. He told me that some years before he had worked twenty hours a day keeping abreast of things and making the right moves. 'That was when Julian was growing up,' he said. 'Naturally I didn't see much of him.'

I nodded and got ready to make my first note. 'How old is he now?'

'Twenty. He joined the army nearly two years ago. He was a champion athlete but he . . . didn't finish school.'

Guyatt was a short, stocky man with a balding head and a high colour. I'll swear he almost blushed when he admitted his offspring was a dropout.

I nodded again. 'Didn't finish the army stint either. Is that his problem, Mr Guyatt? That he can't finish anything?'

'I really don't know. It's a terrible thing to say but I can't claim to know him very well. We hardly spoke in the last years he was at home. Well, he wasn't really at home. He came in for clean shirts and money which his mother gave him.'

'Would you have given them to him?'

'He avoided me. Never came when I was going to be around.'

I sighed. Young Guyatt avoided old Guyatt; old Guyatt avoided questions; I wondered what Mrs Guyatt avoided. 'Was he on good terms with his mother?'

Guyatt nodded.

'What does she have to say about it?'

'She's distraught. She says Julian loved the army and would never desert.'

150

I got a photograph of Julian, the licence number of his blue Laser, a few details on his pre-army life and the last date he had performed his duty at Waterloo Barracks. I also got the telephone number of one Captain Barry Renshaw.

'Step by step, how did it happen?'

'Julian didn't do anything about his mother's birthday. That had never happened before. She rang Waterloo Barracks and was told that he was on leave. That was a lie.'

'How do you know?'

'Julian had told his mother he was going to New Caledonia the next time he got leave, even if it was only for a week. He couldn't have gone. His passport's at home.'

'What then?'

'I rang and was told that my son had been posted as a deserter.'

I looked at my notes. 'You spoke to this Captain Renshaw?'

'No, someone else. I didn't get his name. Renshaw's been handling it since, but we've really heard nothing. Something has to be done.'

'I charge a hundred and fifty dollars a day and expenses,' I said. 'If I work on this for a month you'll be up for over four thousand dollars.'

'Do it. Please.'

I accepted his cheque. After he left, I stared at the photograph until I would have recognised the owner of the strong features, low-growing dark hair and steady eyes anywhere there was enough light to see by. Lately I'd done more debugging and money-minding than I cared for. It was good to have something to do some leg work on. Julian Guyatt hadn't been in the army quite long enough to throw off civilian contacts. I checked at his last two jobs, hung around the pub he'd frequented and spoke to a girl he'd taken out for a few months. The response was the same everywhere: 'Like we told the man from the army, we don't know anything.'

That left Captain Renshaw. I telephoned him and stated my business.

'I don't think I can help you.'

'Don't you want to find him?'

'Of course.' The Captain clipped his words off as if they might straggle and sound untidy.

'I've found a lot of people. I might get lucky.'

'We've tried, so have the police.'

'You and the police have procedures, Captain. You treat all cases the same, cover the same ground. I can treat it as unique. I can feel around and try to find the handle. D'you follow me?'

'One silly young man. I hardly think ... '

'That's what I mean. To his father he's more important than all your Leopard tanks put together. Give me some of your time, anywhere you like, please.'

'I don't know.'

I felt I was losing him. I spoke quickly. 'You tried to find Guyatt by looking into his civilian life, right?'

'Yes.'

'There you go. You need a fresh approach. You're an institutional man and you trust the institution.'

'What do you mean?'

I drew a breath, the next bit was risky. 'I'd check on his army life. Discreetly. I was a soldier myself.'

'Were you? Vietnam?'

'No, Malaya. Don't laugh, I'm not Methuselah. Captain, I'm going to look into this one way or another. I don't leak things to newspapers and I don't write books. Apart from the bare outlines, my files are in my head. You see what I'm getting at?'

'I do. Two o'clock, here at Waterloo Barracks. Suit you?'

I agreed and thanked him. Then I rang Guyatt

and made my meagre report. It didn't sound like a thousand dollars worth to me but Guyatt didn't complain. I asked him about the Laser and he told me that Julian had put a deposit on it and was paying it off from his army pay.

'What finance company?'

'Western, I believe. Madness! I lease, myself.'

I gave my name at a glassed-in, wired-for-sound guardbox. A silent sergeant escorted me down concrete paths, through sturdy metal gates and between some squat, undistinguished red brick boxes to a stylish aluminium and glass block. The sergeant led me down a corridor past some busy offices and knocked on a door marked Military Police.

'Mr Hardy.' A tall, thin man with sparse sandy hair got up from behind a desk and extended his hand. His face was about fifty years old; his uniform looked brand new.

'Captain Renshaw.' We shook hands and I sat in a straight chair by the desk. The room was big enough to hold two other desks, three filing cabinets, a bar fridge and a large bookcase crammed with official-looking publications.

Renshaw pushed a pencil around on the desk in front of him. 'Probably won't surprise you to hear I looked up your record.'

'No,' I said.

'Decent enough. See you don't draw a pension or any benefits. Why's that?'

I shrugged. 'Stubborn. Let's talk about Julian Guyatt. What sort of a soldier is he?'

Renshaw took a file from the top drawer, opened it and ran his eye down the first sheet. 'Pretty good. No apparent weaknesses.'

'Specialist?'

He shook his head. 'No.'

153

'Have you got a psychological profile there? Any progress reports? Anything that suggests a reason for desertion?'

Renshaw kept his eyes on my face. 'Like . . . ?'

'Gambling, drink or drugs, sex?'

'No.'

'Why was Guyatt's mother told he was on leave?'

'A mistake. An apology was made.'

I grinned. 'You're not being a lot of help, Captain. How about a drink?'

He looked puzzled. 'What?'

'There's a fridge behind you. I thought there might be a beer in it.'

He turned his upper body slowly and looked at the fridge as if he was seeing it for the first time. He reached forward and opened it. The seat of the swivel chair moved slightly. The fridge was empty. 'Sorry.'

'Don't worry. I'd like to talk to a couple of his mates.'

Renshaw consulted the file again. 'He doesn't seem to have had any close friends in the service.' He snapped the file shut. 'That's why we looked outside and why I think you're wasting your time. Unless you have any information which could be of help to us.'

I stared at him . . . The temperature in the room seemed to have dropped. Renshaw stood; I heard the sergeant's boots scrape the floor behind me. 'Goodbye, Mr Hardy.'

As an investigative interview it wasn't much to boast about, but I *had* got something. Captain Renshaw didn't know where the fridge was or that his chair swivelled—he hadn't spent more than ten minutes in that office before I arrived. If he was a military policeman I was Frank Sinatra.

I wouldn't say I was encouraged, but at least I had something to bite on. When I checked with the finance company and found that Guyatt's payments had been made for three months ahead, I had a bit more. I did some more phoning—to the police to check on stolen and recovered cars and to a contact who can tell you useful things about credit cards. Result: several Lasers lost and found but not Julian Guyatt's, and he hadn't used his credit cards in the past month.

I slept on it and woke up feeling that I had enough to ring my client and make an appointment to talk to his wife.

The Guyatts lived in Greenwich, which isn't a part of Sydney I know well. I drove there in fine weather in the mid-morning and missed the street because a tree from a front garden was drooping over it. The place seemed to have more trees per square metre than anywhere else east of the Blue Mountains. I found the street and parked outside the long, low, timber house. Some distance off a car backfired and birds flew up from the trees. The noise they made was deafening.

Mrs Guyatt was a large, heavy-featured woman who had given her looks to her son. She seemed commanding and firm of purpose but she was just the opposite. As soon as I mentioned Julian's name her eyes moistened.

'I'll show you his room,' she said.

'I don't think that's necessary.'

She didn't listen. She led me down a passage towards the rear of the house and showed me into a large bedroom that had too much built-in furniture, too much carpet and too much window. It was an ugly room that someone had tried too hard to make comfortable. I stood uncomfortably while Mrs Guyatt showed me Julian's sports trophies— NSW Under-17 100-metres champion, 1984—tennis racquets and skis. There were no books. A poster on the back of the door showed a helicopter gunship in attack, a scene from *Apocalypse Now*.

Down in the over-elaborate sitting room we drank coffee while Mrs Guyatt told me what a good boy her son was.

'Did he have any friends?' I asked.

'Certainly. Chris Petersen, Phil Cash, I'm sure there were others.'

'These are army friends?'

'Yes.'

'Did you try to contact them?'

She looked distressed. 'No. I didn't know how . . .'

'Do you know where they come from, Petersen and Cash, or anyone else he was friendly with?'

'I don't think . . . I believe Phil Cash was from Gundagai. I think Julian said that. Otherwise, no. What has happened?'

'I'm trying to find out. You say you have your son's passport?'

'Yes. Julian left it here after his last trip to New Caledonia. Would you like to see it?'

I said I would. She left the room and came hurrying back, more flustered and distressed than ever. 'It's gone!'

'You're sure. You didn't misplace it?'

'No! I've never misplaced anything of Julian's. How could I? Someone has been in here and taken it.'

I tried to calm her down but didn't do a very good job. In the end I had to phone Guyatt at his office. He said he'd come home but he wasn't pleased at being taken away from his work.

I became aware of the car following me when I was a few miles from the Guyatts'. A grey Corolla. The driver wasn't bad at it but it's almost impossible to follow someone who spots you and doesn't want you there. I lost him in Hunter's Hill between the Lane Cove and Gladesville bridges. I turned off Waterloo

Road towards the city and outlaid some of Guyatt's money in a parking station as close as I could get to the GPO.

The country phone directories were a brand new set. In a few weeks they'd have pages missing and entries obliterated, but for now they were the private detective's friend. There were only three numbers listed for Cash in Gundagai. The woman who answered at the first number had only been in the town a few weeks and gave a squawk of laughter when I asked her if she had a son. 'I'm a lesbian feminist separatist,' she said. 'If I had a son it wouldn't live twenty-four hours.'

The second number was the right one. Mrs Enid Cash confirmed that her son Phillip was in the regular army. 'There hasn't been an accident?' she said anxiously.

'No, nothing like that. I'm Captain Renshaw, Army Statistics. I'm afraid our records haven't been as well kept as they might have been. I'm trying to confirm the rural backgrounds of personnel. They're going to be in line for special benefits.'

'Quite right too. Well, our Phillip grew up on the farm here. He's a country boy.'

'Excellent. Let me see, he's stationed at . . . '

'Waterloo Barracks.'

'Right. He comes home on leave of course?'

'Always.'

'Thank you, Mrs Cash. You don't happen to know anything about a Sergeant Petersen do you?'

'Danny Petersen, do you mean? How exciting! He must've been promoted. Phil will be pleased.'

'Yes. Is he a Gundagai man too?'

'Goodness me, no. He's a Victorian, from Benalla. Phil was always ribbing him about it. But he's from the country too so he'll be eligible, won't he?'

It took me four calls to locate the right Petersen in Benalla, but the story was much the same. Danny was a soldier who always came home on leave. One more call laid it out for me—the duty officer at Waterloo Barracks confirmed that Cash and Petersen were on leave. That would be surprising news to the old folks back home on the farm.

I puzzled about it as I walked through Martin Place back to the car park. I could understand three young men doing something else with their leave than what their mums expected, but the posting of Julian Guyatt as a deserter and Renshaw's manner needed explanation.

I'd parked five or six levels up close to the fire stairs. I had my key in the door lock when the stair door opened and two men came out. I unlocked the door expecting them to go to their car but they suddenly swerved and jumped at me. They were big and quick; one hit me hard and low while the other grabbed my throat with his big, hard hand. He squeezed and I felt the darkness wrapping around me. He eased up and I fought for breath. He squeezed again; the puncher pulled me down so that we were squatting by the car. My knee hit the concrete. The darkness came and went again.

'Let it go, Hardy,' the squeezer said. 'Do yourself a favour and let it go. Understand?'

I shook my head. He put his palm on my forehead and slammed the back of my head against the car door. I felt the metal give.

'Forget about Guyatt or everyone'll forget about you.' He squeezed again and this time the darkness was thick and heavy and it didn't lift.

'The oldest trick in the book,' I said.

'What's that?' A man was brushing me down and helping me to struggle to my feet. I recognised my car; I didn't recognise him.

'You were really out to it,' he said. 'What are you,

a diabetic or an epileptic or something? My aunt
. . .'

I pulled myself up. 'No. I'm all right. Thanks a lot.
I just had a sort of turn. Not enough sleep lately.
Working too hard.'

'Better take it easy.' He moved away, happy to
have helped, happy not to have to help any more.

'Thanks again.' I leaned against the car, massaged my bruised stomach and felt my stiff, aching
neck. It must have been the two car trick; let the
subject see one car following him, drop that one off
and keep him in sight from another. It's not
something I've had much practice at, seeing that I
work alone and can't drive two cars at once. But I
should have thought of it.

I sat in the car for a while until I was sure my head
and vision were clear. My attackers had cost
Ambrose Guyatt some money by delaying me in the
car park.

I reviewed the attack—very fast, very pro-
fessional. If the fist that had hit my belly had
held a knife and the hand that gripped my neck had
gripped harder and longer, it would have been a
classical jungle-fighting kill.

I drove home to Glebe watching for tails and not
spotting any. The cat was outside the house which
wasn't unusual. But when I opened the door it
didn't march straight in ahead of me. That was
unusual. I waited in the passage and listened to the
erratic hum of my refrigerator, the dripping tap in
the bathroom upstairs, the creaking from the loose
piece of roofing iron. All normal. I went in and
looked around. The place had been quickly but
systematically searched.

I made myself a drink and sat down to assemble
what I had. It was a fair bet that my office had been
searched too and if they hadn't found the file that
carried Guyatt's name, his cheque and two or three

other entries, they should go back to searching school. I was in a unique bind: I needed more information on Renshaw, Guyatt, Cash and Petersen. With civilians you can always find a source—a neighbour, a relative, a lover—but these men inhabited a closed world.

The only lead I had into Julian Guyatt's private life was his fondness for New Caledonia. There I had some room to manoeuvre. Ailsa Sleeman, an old friend, has sizeable business interests in New Caledonia and contacts to match. I called her, chatted about old times, and asked her to put out some feelers about Guyatt.

'I'll find out what I can,' she said, 'and you'll have to have a drink with us, Cliff.'

'Us?'

'I'm nearly married again.'

'Don't do it.'

She laughed. 'Maybe I won't.'

I had other things to do for the next few days and I did them. I didn't get in to the office for a couple of days and when I did I found the search had been rougher and more destructive than the one in Glebe. Papers were torn, things were broken and I got angry; my stomach was still sporting a dark bruise. I sat at my desk and brooded. Then I phoned Renshaw.

'Here's what I've got,' I said. 'A deposition from Mrs Guyatt that she was told her son was on leave. A taped conversation with the duty officer to the effect that Cash and Petersen are on leave plus taped conversations from their homes to say they're not. I've got a witness to my being assaulted in the car park and the licence number of a grey Corolla. I've got a video tape of your people searching my office. What d'you say, Captain? Are you going to tell me what's going on?'

Renshaw's short, barking laugh sounded far too confident for my liking. 'You amuse me, Hardy. I'll tell you what you've got—nothing! You called Gundagai and Benalla from a public telephone. Neither of your phones, office or home, has a recording device so you've got no record of any call to the duty officer here. I've never seen you, of course.'

'I've still got a client.'

'Listen, Hardy, I'll talk freely since I know you can't record anything I say. I'll admit that clumsy mistakes have been made. That's all I'll admit.'

'I don't think that'll satisfy Guyatt.'

Renshaw was calm, almost courtly. 'I think it will. I think his good lady's satisfied too. Why don't you ask them? Goodbye, Hardy.'

I've heard that tone of voice before; it's the tone of the fixer, the smoother-out of things who feels that he's done a good job. I drove to Guyatt's place of business in North Sydney. It was a busy operation —warehouse, printery and machine division topped by an office space that seemed to be in the process of expanding. I fronted up to a reception desk and told the young woman in charge that I wanted to see Ambrose Guyatt.

'Yes, he's . . . oh, have you got an appointment?'

Something about her manner and the bustle of the place suggested newness, innovation. 'I've never needed an appointment to see Ambrose before,' I said. 'What's up?'

She leaned forward confidentially. 'You haven't heard?'

'No,' I whispered.

The phone rang and she fumbled uncertainly with the buttons on the new-looking system. When she got the call properly placed she smiled at me. 'New contract. Big one.'

I felt a lurch in my stomach, just below the bruise. 'Oh, the army thing?'

'Yes, isn't it wonderful? Hey!'

I walked past the desk and pushed open the door she'd been guarding. Ambrose Guyatt sat with a phone at his ear in front of a paper-strewn desk. He was smiling as he spoke into the instrument. The smile faded as he saw me come into the room. He spoke quickly and hung up.

'Hardy.'

'Mr Guyatt.'

He reached into a drawer of his desk and took out an envelope. 'What's that?' I said.

He beckoned me closer. 'Cash instead of the cheque,' he said softly.

I was standing beside the desk now, looking down at him. His thin, dark hair was freshly cut and he was wearing a new suit. I took the envelope. 'Congratulations on the army contract.'

He nodded.

'Want to tell me where Julian is?'

'I can't.'

'Secret mission? Something like that?'

'I can't say a word.'

'I understand his mother's a proud and happy woman?'

His eyes widened as a faint doubt crept in. 'I think you'd better go.'

'I will. I'm sorry for you, Mr Guyatt. You're going to be a very unhappy man.'

'What . . . what d'you mean?'

I leaned close to him. I could smell his expensive aftershave and the aroma of cigar smoke. 'They don't make these arrangements for things that go right, Mr Guyatt. They do it for things that go wrong.'

He gaped at me as I walked out of the office.

I was right. Ailsa reported to me several days later. The information was fragmentary, hardly to be relied upon unless you had something to support it as I had. Julian Guyatt was part of a small task force that had been infiltrated into New Caledonia to operate against the Kanaks. It had been wiped out in the first exchange. Piecing it all together, the one-time Under-17 100-metres champion had been dead for twenty-four hours when his father first stepped into my office.

Byron Kelly's Big Mistake

THE newspaper Byron Kelly dumped on my desk carried the headline DECOMPOSED BODY IN PARK. That made it a fairly ordinary day in Sydney, but Byron hadn't come to talk about bodies or parks or for help with the crossword.

'I've got to get it back, Cliff,' he said. 'or she'll ruin me and a lot of others. This time, she doesn't know what she's doing.'

It was late on a Tuesday morning in March. We were in my office in St Peter's Lane, Darlinghurst. Byron was looking a bit crumpled in his expensive clothes. He moved restlessly from the chair to lean on the filing cabinet and try to look through the dirty window. I sat behind my desk; I was less expensive but less crumpled and I knew there was no point in trying to look out the windows.

'What exactly are we talking about, mate?' I said. 'A letter, a memo, a rocket fuel formula, what?'

'A letter, no, a draft letter,' Byron said. 'Michael roughed out a letter to . . . one of the money men who'd approached him about getting the all-clear for a development. Two things, no three. One, Michael was pissed at the time; two, he thought he was going to get the Department of the Environment and three, it was a bloody joke anyway.'

'And you showed the letter to Pauline. I suppose you were pissed at the time too?'

'No. Just angry. It was a bad time for us. The point is, she took it and she's been saying all over town that she intends to fry me and this had to be the way she's going to do it.'

'What do you want me to do?'

'Talk to her.'

'I'm a private detective, not a marriage guidance counsellor.'

'You're also my friend.'

'And hers. Don't forget that.'

'Jesus! You know what it's been like with us, Cliff. We love each other and all that but it's impossible. She's done this before, used stuff I've shown her against me but . . .'

'Why d'you show her?'

'I don't know. Rage, I guess. But this is bigger. There's some very heavy people behind this development and it's going through for better or worse.'

'Where?'

'Albion Reef, up north. Lovely spot. Was. This'll fuck it but there's jobs and money at stake. It just squeaked through an environmental impact study— took some modifications and some palm greasing. You know how it is.'

I grunted. 'What was in Parsons' letter?'

'Enough dirt on the developers and the graft to sink it. The silly bastard really let himself go. If it gets out the development's gone, Parsons is gone and I'm gone. The government'll probably survive.'

'Does Pauline know all the ramifications?'

'Probably not. She certainly wouldn't know exactly who's putting up the real money.'

'You're sure she's got the letter?'

'Has to be. She's got a key to the flat I moved into.'

'Why's that?'

Byron pushed his thick brown hair back and looked boyish although he's in his thirties and has knocked around. 'I didn't want anything to look too final.'

'You want her back?'

He shrugged. 'It's fantastic with her when it's good. Unbelievable. Then these things come up and it's hell. I don't know.'

'Have you tried to talk to her about the letter?'

'She hangs up. I tried to catch her in at the *News*. She went into the women's dunny. I waited, then I went in. She'd left by another door. Look, I'm not only worried about the flak. That letter's dangerous. The big noise is . . .'

I held up my hand. 'Don't tell me. I don't want to know. Let me think.'

I'd known Byron and Pauline Kelly for eight years. For most of that time they'd been married, that is, all except a few months at the beginning and the last few weeks since they separated. They fought. At the beginning they were known as Rocky II; that was before the movie came out. Since then they've been Rocky III, IV, as the movies caught up with them. They'd called it off several times but the current separation looked final. Rocky V, at least their version, seemed unlikely.

Byron was Michael Parsons' political adviser cum press secretary cum bodyguard cum drinking companion. Parsons was rising fast in the state political zoo. He was currently a Minister but I wasn't quite certain what for.

Pauline was a journalist, an in-demand freelance who appeared in print, on radio and on television. Byron was a pragmatist, Pauline an idealist; they agreed on almost nothing but the superiority of red wine over white. Pauline had once told me why they stayed together.

'Because of King Arthur.'

'What?' I said.

'We come a lot.'

Pauline was a small woman, blonde, untidy and energetic. I liked her. Byron was a foot taller, more careful of his appearance but somehow always in her shadow. I liked him too so it pained me to see him looking strained and underslept. 'How come you kept this letter?' I said. 'Why didn't you get rid of it when your boss was sober?'

'You don't understand what it's like working for these blokes. Pauline didn't understand either. They're like ... shit, I don't know. Have you ever been to a really even fight, where the fighters slugged it out all night and finished up square?'

'Sure. Rose and Famechon.'

Kelly scratched his head. 'They never fought.'

'That's what it would've been like if they had.'

'Okay. Well, these politicians get off a lot of shots; they torpedo people and humiliate them but they're sitting ducks themselves. Real targets. If they make the wrong move at the wrong time, they're history.'

'My heart bleeds all over their superannuation cheques.'

'You sound like Pauline. I find it sort of exciting. Parsons's not a bad bloke. Compared to the guy on the other side he's a genius and a saint rolled into one, but he's got his faults. He gets pissed at a certain pressure level. I kept the letter to scare him, to show him what political suicide looks like. I didn't get around to doing that. I showed it to Pauline when we were having one of our blues and ... that's it.'

'Does Parsons know the letter's floating around?'

'Christ no!'

'Why me, Byron?'

'You like Pauline. Not everybody does. She likes you and ... '

'Not everybody does,' I said.

Byron grinned. 'You'd know. Look, Cliff, I have to play this close to the chest. Almost everybody I know has a word processor. They write everything down. They're all keeping diaries, for Christ's sake. It needs ... discretion.'

'She'll know I've talked to you. She might be hard to catch up with.'

'Right.'

'A hundred and fifty a day and expenses.'

'Jesus!'

'Discretion guaranteed.'

Kelly grimaced and put on his very good American accent, a legacy of his time at UCLA. 'You got it.'

After he left I spent a few minutes thinking about how unwise it was to get involved in a separated couple tangle. *Certain disaster, bound to lose one friend if not two.* But business was business, angry men exaggerate and Pauline might have calmed down. I gave myself enough reasons to pick up the phone and ring the house in Willoughby where I assumed Pauline was still living.

The voice in the answering machine was breathy and cigarette-choked: 'This is Pauline Lyons. I'm out at the moment. Please leave a message after the beep and I'll get back to you. If it's Byron Kelly calling or anyone connected with him ... don't bother!'

A challenge. I said: 'Pauline, it's Cliff Hardy. I want to talk to you. Please ring me—you know the numbers.'

I hung up and waited. The call came through in about as long as it must have taken her to ring my home number before the office one.

'What do you want?' she said.

'Aha, you leave your machine on broadcast and listen to the messages.'

'Who doesn't? What's on your mind, Cliff? If you want a fuck I might be interested. In fact that's the only reason I'm talking to you.'

'At least you're talking.'

'Make it quick, I'm on my way out.'

'I want Michael Parsons' letter.'

'Shit, that again. I don't know anything about it. I barely glanced at it. I was too pissed to take any notice. I told Byron a hundred times.'

'He's worried about you, he . . . '

'Bullshit!'

'How about the fuck then?'

'I think I'll wait for someone keener.' She hung up hard.

It isn't that Pauline tells lies exactly, it's just that she regards journalism as one of the highest callings and the freedom of the press as a sacred human right. She'd say Joh Bjelke-Petersen made sense if she had to in defence of her trade. I've met people like her before—stiff-necked lilywhites. There's only two ways to go—front up and convince them that what *you* want is really best for them, or sneak behind their backs and steal it.

I used a credit card to buy a tank of petrol because I don't like to carry that much cash and drove out to Willoughby. The house was a medium-sized, middle-aged timber and glass job that was usually as messy as a garden shed. Byron and Pauline used to say that the dullness of Willoughby was just what they needed after the excitements of politics and journalism.

I was there within half an hour of the phone call. For a top flight journalist Pauline was incredibly disorganised. I judged that 'now' meant in ten minutes, 'soon' meant half an hour and 'on my way' could mean almost anything. I parked down the street, listened to a news broadcast. Another body had turned up, naked, dead for some time and as yet unidentified. The report linked the two deaths through the police statement that the men were 'well nourished'. To be thin was getting healthier all the time.

Pauline's Gemini backed out of the drive and roared off in the direction of the city.

In a two-income belt nothing stirs in the early afternoon. The Kellys have a German Shepherd named Gough who looks as if he'd tear your throat out but is as gentle as a lamb if you know him. I opened the front gate and walked towards the house on an overgrown pebble path; Gough loped up to greet me.

I patted his head. 'Hello, Gough,' I said. 'Nothing will save the Governor-General.' He growled amiably and watched me squint in the gloom of the heavily tree-shaded porch as I picked the lock of the front door.

Byron's departure had brought changes in the house—some books and pictures were missing, the furniture was extensively rearranged and the small room that had served as his study was empty. Pauline had worked in the room that also served as a spare bedroom. It was chaotic as usual, with books and papers spilling everywhere, brimming ashtrays, sticky glasses and coffee cups, half-eaten sandwiches, forgotten biscuits.

Chaos is harder to search through than order; I spent more than an hour there, patiently sifting and probing. As far as I could tell Pauline was working on three different stories and a novel. The stories were about police corruption, religious sects in Queensland gaols and a profile of a newly appointed judge. The novel was about a terrorist who was laying mines in Sydney Harbour.

Pauline was famous for the depth of her research, even on small stories. There wasn't a scrap of evidence to suggest that she had any interest in a land development on the central coast.

I picked up one of the sandwiches and a couple of the biscuits and fed them to Gough on the way out.

When I got back to Glebe there were three frantic messages from Kelly on my answering machine. I phoned him and had to tell him to calm down and take a breath and stop gabbling.

'Okay, okay,' he said. 'You've got to see Pauline. She's in danger.'

'I saw her an hour ago. She was a danger to others the way she was driving.'

'Stop fucking joking! You heard about the second body?' His voice was thick with worry and fear.

'Yeah,' I said. 'Unidentified.'

'Not any more. Not if you know who to talk to. That means two of the characters associated with this development I was telling you about are dead.'

'What sort of characters?'

'Operators, you know the kind. I didn't make anything of it when the first one turned up. The cops sat on it but I got a whisper on who he was. Name of Morrison. He was a go-between, handled the graft, or some of it. Michael mentioned him in the letter. Well, those blokes—they're into all sorts of things. They have enemies. But this new one, Brent Fuller. Shit!'

'He in the letter too?'

'Yeah. He was more ... central and more ... exposed. Am I making sense?'

'Only just.'

'In a thing like this there's always a couple of unreliable people. Michael's letter pointed out a few weak links. Pauline must've showed the letter to someone who's in with them, or talked about it.'

'You're sure you didn't talk to anyone? There aren't any copies?'

'No. Copies? Don't be crazy. It looks to me as if they're getting rid of a few of the expendable people. Look, in effect, they've taken out number one and two among the small fry if you regard Michael's letter as a sort of list.'

'How well do you know these people?'

'Parsons knows ... knew Fuller pretty well. I knew him too.'

'You should be talking to number three.'

'I have. They almost got him this morning. They killed his guard dog but they tripped an alarm. He's on a plane right now.'

'Where would Pauline have been going? I saw her leave your house.'

'The *News* most likely. I called but she's set up some kind of interference system. I can't get through to her. I'm worried, Cliff.'

'Yeah. Where're you now?'

'Balmain. At my flat.'

'It's time for the cops, Byron. Whatever the consequences.'

'Jesus. Yeah, I suppose so.'

'I'll take Pauline somewhere safe and I'll call you. You've got a bit of time to think about it but ... '

'I'll do it. Don't worry. Just get her!'

I drove in to the newspaper building, parked illegally and took a lift to the features office where Pauline did her talking and filing. The editor told me that she'd gone off to the pub, the Colonial nearby, with some fellow workers. I reached the pub in record time and spotted Pauline drinking in a corner of the saloon bar. I went across and grabbed her arm.

'Pauline, I've got to talk to you.'

'Piss off.' She jerked her arm free and some of her drink spilled on the trousers of the heavy-set man on the opposite stool. Pauline giggled; it wasn't her first drink. 'Sorry, Stan. I'll get your pants dry-cleaned if you'll take them off.'

Stan smiled and lifted his glass. I jolted his arm trying to get another grip on Pauline and his drink spilled down his shirt.

'Shit! What the fuck d'you think you're doing?'

Pauline laughed. 'Stan, defend my honour.'

Stan came off his stool faster than I expected. He

was big and thick and moved like a footballer rather than a boxer but he connected on my shoulder with a solid swinging right. I had to let go of Pauline to keep my balance.

'Keep out of this, you,' I snarled. 'Pauline, this isn't a joke, Byron . . .'

'Bugger Byron! And bugger you, too.'

Maybe that was what Stan had been waiting to hear. Stan was certainly eager. He slammed me in the chest and got set to take my head off with another swing. I stepped back, drew him forward and belted him with a quick left hook to the ear. The three or four other drinkers around craned forward interestedly. Pauline shouted something that might have been 'Stop!' or might have been 'Go!' I didn't pay proper attention because Stan was in again, swinging. I fended two shots off with my forearms and stepped closer bringing my heel hard down on his toe. He yelped and I uppercut him so that his teeth clicked. He stumbled back and went down.

I gripped Pauline's arm and pulled her off the stool. 'Don't talk. Just come!'

'You *are* keen, after all,' she said.

I hauled her to the car and drove to Glebe. When she was settled with a drink I called Kelly's flat and got no answer.

'That's odd.'

Pauline raised her glass. 'He's odd. Did you know he's kinky? Likes to dress up.'

I stared at her. 'I don't believe it.'

She giggled. 'You're right. He doesn't. I do. Wanna play, Cliff?'

'I want you to stay here while I go and find out what's happened.'

'Happened? Whaddya mean happened? Nothing happens to Byron, nothing happens anywhere near Byron, he . . .'

'Shut up, Pauline. This is serious. Two people

173

Parsons wrote about in that letter are dead. Byron's scared you could be next.'

'I'm sick of hearing about that fucking letter! I hardly looked at it.' She stopped as if her own words had made an impact on her. She stared at me, trying to focus. 'Two people dead? You mean some of the shit might actually be rubbing off on Parsons?'

'Maybe, but Byron . . . '

'Hold on. I'm going to freshen up. This sounds interesting.'

She went to the bathroom and came back dabbing at her face with a towel. 'It sounds like a story. I suppose Byron's told you I've used confidential stuff?'

I nodded.

'I haven't. He's paranoid. You said something's happened. What?'

'I'm going to Balmain to find out.'

'Me too.'

'You're pissed.'

'I sober up fast. I'm coming.'

There was no point in arguing. We got back in the car. Pauline lit a cigarette, took deep drags and seemed to be trying to will herself sober. When she finished the cigarette she wound the window down and breathed deeply. She coughed and looked red and sore-eyed but her voice was steadier.

'Two dead, you said. You mean the bodies, last night and this morning?'

'Yeah.' I made the turn into Darling Street. 'Morrison, I think it was, and . . . Fuller. Byron knew them.'

'Jesus. Fuller got Byron his flat. He's into real estate around here and Byron wanted a place in Balmain. You know how it works.'

I did. I knew that the politicians and their associates were involved in a network of favours and obligations, given and granted, that to some extent governed what they did. Some of them were 'covered', as the smart operators put it, by girls, gambling debts, shonky deals. There were a hundred ways.

Byron's flat was in Duke Place where town-houses are going up as fast as they can pull the old warehouses and chandlers' sheds down. I parked and twisted the steering wheel so the car wouldn't roll into Mort Bay. Old habit. The handbrake on my newish Falcon is rock solid. Pauline got slowly and stiffly from the car and stumbled in her high heels as she crossed the road.

'You all right?' I said. 'I understand you've got a key to this place. You can show me the way. I was only here once at night.'

'I've never been here. I never used his stupid key.'

'Got it with you?'

We walked along a pebbled path and skirted some freshly planted silver birch trees. I had a vague idea of the block Byron was in. Pauline produced a key from her bag. 'A8,' she read from the tag. 'He said it's got a nice view. I swore I'd never come here.'

I looked for the block numbers. 'Why?'

'It's a mistake. We're finished!'

'I doubt it.'

I got my bearings and we went up a steep set of concrete steps that took us to a sloping walkway leading to the upper level of the block. Kelly's flat was at the end, the most elevated and with the best view of the water, the ships and the container dock. I gave it a glance while Pauline handed me the key. I had my Smith & Wesson .38 under my arm and I got it out before I opened the door.

'What's wrong?' Pauline said.

'I don't know.' I unlocked the door and pushed it open. Nothing happened, no shouts, no shots, no cries of welcome. I edged in half a metre, keeping close to the wall, and looking and listening hard.

175

There was nothing to hear and only some scuff marks and wet stains on the polished wood floor to see.

'Byron!' Pauline shouted.

Nothing. We went into the flat. It was sparsely furnished and scarcely lived in. The big room that served as a living and eating and music and view-absorbing space was neat except for an overturned chair, a coffee table pulled askew and a shattered Swedish upright lamp. I stood there and looked at the signs while Pauline rushed into the other rooms.

She joined me beside the broken lamp. 'What's happened?' she said.

I bent and examined the stains on the floor. They were dark, wet, fresh. 'He's been taken.'

'Taken?'

I pointed to the faint, irregular dust marks. 'He was hit. Showed some fight. Maybe hit a couple of times. They rolled him in a rug.'

'They? Who?'

I followed the marks and stains back down the passage to the door. The stains stopped at the door; there was a flattened bush ten metres directly below in the garden. One shoe lay on the freshly cut grass. Pauline bent over the rail to look.

'No,' she said.

I held her as her legs went rubbery and helped her back into the flat. She was crying hard and rubbing her clenched fists in her eyes. I put her on the couch and went to the phone which was on a table by a sliding window. The balcony outside gave a view of Sydney to gladden a real estate agent's heart. The water sparkled, the boats looked clean and the bridge was a noble arch. There were trees growing down to the water in some places and even the industrial bits looked dignified. Not what Captain Arthur Phillip would have seen but not bad. I put my gun down and lifted the phone.

I heard it as the phone responded to the punched buttons. A faint feedback; a hum so soft you wouldn't hear it if you were breathing hard or scratching your nose. The phone in the flat, which the late Fuller, who was tied in to the Albion Reef development, had procured for Kelly was bugged. I looked back down the passage towards the door and wondered how many people had keys to it besides Byron and Pauline. I could spend some time and money on it, probably come up with some names, but I knew that Michael Parsons had had his last briefing and Pauline had had her last fight and I'd had my last drink with Byron Kelly.

Norman Mailer's Christmas

HENRY Quinn was a burly man with grey curly hair and a face that had been shaped by good days and bad nights, booze and a fair amount of self-admiration. He looked a lot like Norman Mailer and he was aware of the resemblance. A shelf in his study carried a large photograph of Mailer and hard-cover copies of the books, from *The Naked and the Dead* to the latest best-seller. There are people who say Mailer isn't subtle; that's nothing compared to Quinn—there were no other books in the study.

Quinn leaned back in his leather chair and swilled the brandy in his glass. 'You see it, hey? The likeness? Boy, have I had some fun with that.'

It was midday; I'd refused Quinn's offer of brandy and was drinking beer. 'Have you read the books?'

'No. Never had the time. But lemme tell you. I'm on a plane see? An' these up-country types 're lookin' at me and I know what they're thinkin'. They're whispering an' then one of 'em gets up the nerve to talk to me. Know what I say?'

I shook my head. I didn't want to know but he'd called and said he had a job for me and that he'd pay for my time from the minute I'd said 'Hardy Investigations' into the phone. So he'd paid for me to drive to Cronulla and to drink with him in his penthouse with its northerly ocean view on a beautiful summer day. I owed him a hearing.

'I say: "I'm not who you think I am," and they're hooked, see? After that they eat outa my hand and I sign anything they give me. Sign it Norman M. It makes their day. Hah, hah.'

I shifted uneasily in the chair—too deep, too soft,

more like marshmallow than leather. 'So Mailer's threatened to punch you or have you punched and you need protection. That it?'

'Nah, nah. Him'n me'd get on fine, I'm sure. I'm a Brooklyn boy myself, well, Jersey. Close enough. Nah. I got a wife problem. I had three.'

'I think Mailer tops you there.'

'Right, right. And I never knifed one neither, though God knows I woulda liked to. But now, I wanna bury the hatchet. Get the girls all together on Christmas, have a few drinks, a few laughs. Show I'm a big guy. Hell, I'm thinking of gettin' married again an' I'd like a clean slate.'

'Where are they all—Reno?'

'What?' He looked disconcerted for the first time but he recovered fast. He laughed and shook his head so that the curls floated around. It was a much practised movement. 'Nah, nah. All Aussie girls. I been here since '56. Came over for the Olympics. I was on the US boxing team, light heavy.'

'How'd you do?'

'Lousy, got disqualified for gougin' in the first fight.'

'You was robbed, I suppose?'

He grinned. The sun had moved and with some more light falling on his face I could see that he'd had a lot of work done on his teeth and some on his nose. Maybe he'd given the surgeon the picture of Norman to work from. 'Nah. I went for his eye all right. We played it a bit rougher Stateside. But I liked the country an' the people so I came back. Went inna business.' He waved his hand around the room with the view. 'Did okay.'

'Mm. Well, the wives . . .?'

'Can't locate one of 'em—Shelley.' He reached behind him, took a large, glossy photograph from the top of the bar fridge and passed it to me. 'Good looker, eh, mate?'

His phony Australian accent was excruciating but

Shelley fitted the description. She was a brunette in her twenties with bushy, wild hair, slanted eyes and a generous smile. 'Got the other wives lined up, have you, Mr Quinn?'

'Call me Henry. Man drinks with me, works for me, he calls me Henry. Secret of my success. Yeah, Francine an' Dawn are all set. They're bringing their guys along, no, Dawn is. Francine's a lezzie though you coulda fooled me at the time. Know what I mean? Hah, hah.'

It was December 20, not long to find someone for a Christmas party. On the other hand it was about as long as I'd care to work for Mr Quinn. 'A hundred and fifty a day and expenses. Half up front.'

Quinn nodded, reached for his wallet and extracted notes. 'Give you a grand now, another grand if you find her, quits if you don't. This is important to me, Hardy. Serious. So I'm putting up serious money.'

'Fair enough. I'll need a smaller photo, names, addresses and dates.'

'An' another beer,' Quinn said. 'Hah, hah.'

Quinn gave me what I asked for—a snapshot-sized photograph, the name of the last place his ex-wife had worked and her last home address. Their divorce had been finalised six months before and he hadn't been in touch with her since. He also gave me a sealed envelope for her which he said contained an invitation to the Christmas party. I rode the lift twelve floors down to the lobby and walked through the plush reception area with the potted palms and the mirrors thinking that the job stank.

Why the short notice? Why not put an ad in a paper? Why not go through Shelley's solicitor? But in this business you can't be too choosy, especially in the holiday season when things are slow. I had a mortgage to meet, car repair bills, credit card instalments and I also liked to eat and drink once in a while. Outside the day was almost as perfect as it had looked from the penthouse. The air was clear after a wet, windy couple of days and the promise of a long, golden year's end and year's beginning was showing on the sea and the sand and in people's faces.

The addresses helped me to make my decision. Shelley Quinn had worked the previous summer as a water skiing instructor at a health club at Narrabeen and her most recent address was Whale Beach. Not hard places to take at that time of year. Swimming costume country, suntan territory. But first I needed to make sure that Henry Quinn wasn't CIA or the Mafia.

I drove back to Glebe and opened all the windows in my house to catch a breeze that had a faint salty tang to it as well as some chemical and industrial smells. There was no need to steam open the letter. It was a plain envelope and the name was type-written, easily duplicated. Inside was a white card with gold lettering on it. It invited Shelley Quinn to 'drinks to celebrate Christmas' at noon. The place was the penthouse and the scrawled initials were HQ. I sipped a glass of white wine and looked out into my backyard which, ever since Hilde planted the herbs and put in the ivy and the pots, could be called a courtyard. The cardboard boxes with the empties and the yellowed metre-high stack of newspapers were my own touch.

I held the card up to the light. *What did you expect?* I thought. A death threat? He wants to have a drink with his ex-wives, wouldn't you like to have a drink with yours, with Cyn? How about Ailsa and Kay Fletcher and a couple of others? I knew I'd hate it, but then I wasn't like Quinn who seemed to be one of those people who only believed in his own existence. To the Quinns of the world, life without Quinn is unthinkable.

I put my drink beside the telephone and made some calls about my employer to people whose business it is to know people in business. Quinn checked out as only slightly grubby: he'd made money in a variety of ways—interstate trucking in the early, rough days, swimming pool manufacturing, land development. One of my informants, a banker with a conscience, said that Quinn might have some problems with the US Treasury.

'He moves money around a bit. Dodgy from the US point of view. But his Australian resident alien status protects him.'

'How did he come by that?'

'Our file says by marriage to one Dawn Leonie Simkin.'

'Since divorced.'

'That doesn't revoke it. He's been pretty quick on his feet in this country. If they passed some retrospective tax laws he'd be in trouble, but otherwise he's okay here.'

Which left me not liking Mr Quinn any more but not liking his money any less. It was late in the day by the time I'd finished phoning. I spent the night at home writing cheques, reading and watching a tape of the day's tennis on television. As an addicted sports fan will, I checked on the light heavyweight division in the 1956 Olympics. The gold was won by James M. Floyd which didn't mean much. It was different the next time round—Cassius M. Clay won in Rome in 1960.

The next day was a Sydney summer special—there was a light breeze and a freshness in the air at 7am but you could feel the heat building. I was at the health club at Narrabeen soon after 9am. The big expanse of water which everyone calls a lake is really a lagoon; its shores feature most of the possible natural features from thick timber to sparse, rocky beaches. The Peninsula Health Club spread over several hectares of paddocks, tennis courts, swimming pools and aluminium and glass buildings that housed a gymnasium, squash courts, spas, saunas and a kitchen which seemed to be totally given over to the production of carrot juice.

I got a lot of this information from a pamphlet I was given to read while I waited for my credentials to be checked at the security gate. Things have changed in the affluent parts of Sydney in recent times. There's more paranoia, less relaxation. To get to talk to anyone at this place I had to present my operator's licence, give a police reference, details of my bonding and the name of my lawyer. I was getting used to this insecurity, slowly.

Mr James Lewis was the security manager and he eventually consented to talk to me. He was a big, fit-looking man in his fifties who met me on the gravel path inside the gate. The path led to the water which was blue and inviting. Mr Lewis said he didn't have an office.

'Offices are the enemy of fitness, Hardy,' he said. 'We've got everything we need to know here on a computer. I can use it but I don't need to sit at a desk. I walk around. If you want to talk to me you have to walk.'

'Fair enough. Looks like a great place.' I was glad I was wearing only light shoes, jeans and a cotton shirt. The air was clear and warm; insects buzzed in the grass and some water birds took off from the surface of the lake and wheeled away over the trees.

'It is. Now, what's your business?'

'I have a client who wants to spend some time here. She has certain ... health problems. She wants first class treatment and total security.'

'She'll get it here.' He picked up a stone and sent it skipping over the water.

I gave him one of my sceptical smiles. 'That's what you say. She wants to hear me say it. She likes to water ski.'

Lewis was a man of few words. He made a motion

with his head in the direction of a jetty where five sleek speedboats were bobbing in the water. 'Top facilities.'

I could cut down on syllables too. 'Instructors?'

'The best.'

'Mind if I talk to one? Lady ... my client has some queries.'

We strolled over to where two young women in bathing suits were checking the water ski equipment. They were like peas in a pod—blonde, deeply tanned and with long, whippy muscles.

'Louise and ah ... ?' Lewis said.

Blonde Two pushed up her sunglasses. 'Jenny. Hi.'

'Hello.'

'Come to ski?'

I shook my head. Lewis had stood still for some seconds and he didn't seem to like it. He bounced on his heels and walked off towards the boats.

'I'm a private detective,' I said. 'I'm looking for Shelley Quinn.'

'Shit,' Blonde One said. 'I thought you might be looking for fun. Shelley's not here anymore. She quit right at the end of the season.'

'Why, d'you know?'

'Sure. She was pregnant.'

If I hadn't been wearing sunglasses she'd have seen me blinking in surprise. She couldn't miss the dropped jaw. 'She was divorced.'

'You really aren't any fun!' Blonde Two pulled down her sunglasses in agreement. They started checking a pile of life jackets.

'Is she still at Whale Beach?'

Blonde One sighed. 'Last I saw her was at Manly.'

Lewis was coming back from the boats. 'Where at Manly?' I hissed.

'Tim's Gym, aerobics. C'mon Jen, obstructions check.'

Lewis nodded as the women ran past him. 'Satisfied?'

'What's an obstructions check?'

'Oh, they make sure there's no logs or debris in the water. Your client'll be safe here, Mr Hardy.'

'I'll tell him . . . her.'

That earned me a suspicious look from Lewis and a polite version of the bum's rush.

I drove up the Peninsula and checked the Whale Beach address just to be thorough. The house was on a cliff overlooking the sea. Great view, but it had been occupied for seven months by a body-surfing accountant who worked from home. The previous occupiers' names were Quinn and Buck. A few letters for them had arrived and the accountant had no forwarding address. I drove to Manly wondering who Buck might be.

Tim's Gym was a few streets back from the ocean beach on the south side of The Corso. It was on a hill and from where I parked I could see down across the buildings to the water. The sun was high now and the people were clustering in the shade of beach umbrellas and the trees. All except the joggers who moved in a thin, bobbing trickle along the path that led around to Shelly Beach. What with the joggers and the gym, with its big mural of dancers, weight-lifters and rope-skippers, I experienced an oppressive sense of good health all about me. I would've liked a swim; I'd have liked a drink even more.

Manly has retained more of the flavour of old Australia, where if you asked questions about people you were a sticky-beak but not necessarily an enemy and if you had anything to hide you were a crook. That still didn't make it a pushover. I asked for Tim and was shown to an office where a woman with red hair, a white dress and perfect teeth was operating a desktop computer.

'I'm Sally Teale,' she said. 'There's no Tim. What can I do for you?'

I pulled out the photograph of Shelley Quinn and showed it to her. 'D'you know this woman?'

'I might. Who wants to know?'

'My name's Hardy. I'm a private investigator.' I showed her my licence. 'I know it sounds silly but I've been hired to locate her and invite her to a Christmas party.'

She laughed; the teeth appeared to be perfect all the way back. 'That's not very macho, is it?'

I laughed too. 'No, not very.'

'Hired by who?'

'Her ex-husband.'

'Well, well. Shelley said he was a touch on the sedentary side. I suppose it's all right but I don't know how Peter'll take to it.'

'Peter?'

'Peter Buck. Her bloke.'

I shrugged. 'No business of mine. If you'll give me her address I'll go around and give this to her.' I produced the envelope. 'Or I might just leave it in the letter box.'

I waited for the objection but none came. She hit some keys on the computer which whirred. She looked at the screen of the monitor, nodded and read: 'Flat 3, 42A Darley Road. Not far for you to go.'

'When did you last see her, Ms Teale?'

'Yesterday. She's getting back into shape after having the baby. Lovely little kid.'

Down the hill, around a few turns, and brakes on outside a cream brick block of flats numbered 42A. Easy money. I had my swimmers in the back of the car; maybe I could be on a wave within the hour. I located Flat 3 at the side of the building and went up the short flight of steps. This put me on a concrete porch with a waist high iron rail around it outside a

186

plain door with an electric bell. I pressed the bell and heard movement inside. The door opened and the woman whose photograph was in my pocket stood there.

'Yes?'

'Mrs Quinn? Your former husband . . . '

'The name's Buck.' A man appeared from behind her; he was stocky and dark in shorts and a blue singlet. A man of action; he stepped around the woman, moved forward and threw a punch. Having to move sideways first threw him off line a little, otherwise the punch would've been hard to avoid. But I had time to go back, take it on the shoulder and grab his arm.

'Steady, you! What're you doing?' He jerked free, set himself and punched again. This time he landed under the ear and inspired the standard Hardy counter—I hit him with a light left to the nose and tried to shove him back against something hard. The woman screamed which seemed to give him extra strength. He rushed me back and I felt the rail bite into my spine. I turned to reduce the impact and kicked at his knee as he came on. He wobbled and I put both hands on his right shoulder and bore down. The knee I'd kicked hit the concrete hard and he yelled and crumpled up.

The woman bent down to him and then a baby wailed inside the flat. She rushed in and I moved to follow. The dark man pulled himself up on the railing.

'Get out!' he yelled.

'Easy, mate,' I said. 'You've got some wrong ideas.'

I went into the passageway and Shelley Quinn or Buck came out carrying and soothing a baby. 'Who are you?'

'My name's Hardy. I was hired by your husband to . . . '

187

'That bastard! I'll kill you!' The man hobbled forward.

'You didn't do so good the first time. Don't push your luck. Let's go inside and talk. I don't understand this.'

I stood aside and let him pass me; he held on to the door and edged along the wall. As I closed the door I saw a green car pull up outside the flats. I had a sudden alarmed feeling that I'd seen it before.

We went through to the kitchen. Shelley made coffee and we stumbled through the introductions and explanations. The child was Henry Quinn's but neither Shelley nor Peter Buck wanted anything to do with the father. Shelley snorted when I showed her the invitation.

'He's an animal,' she said. 'I wouldn't go to a party there without a suit of armour.'

'He . . . beat her up,' Peter Buck said hesitantly. 'She wouldn't let me go around and square him.' He had work-hardened hands and muscles but was extraordinarily gentle when handling the child. He was part Maori and he sang when he could and laboured when he couldn't. The chemistry between Buck and Shelley was strong and the child, dark-eyed and olive-skinned, could have been their own. It was clear that that was how they regarded him.

Shelley explained that she'd met and married Quinn as a piece of youthful folly. She'd begun divorce proceedings within a year and had moved to Whale Beach. Quinn broke in and raped her.

'He wants Tommy,' Shelley said quietly. 'That's why you're here. It has to be.'

It dawned on me then. The green car and the feeling I'd had all along that Quinn's story was shonky. I'd approached it all too lightly and hadn't once looked to see if anyone was taking an interest in me. 'Can you see the back and the front of the block from this flat?'

Peter Buck nodded. He rubbed his knee and glowered at me. 'Why?'

'Would you mind taking a look? I think I've led Quinn straight to you.'

He hobbled away and when he came back his face was grim. 'There's cars back and front. Blokes in 'em. They're watching.'

Shelley caught her breath and hugged the baby who protested. She smoothed the soft, dark hair. 'What can we do?'

I phoned Quinn and could hear the satisfaction in his voice. 'Thought I'd be hearing from you. My men're outside those scumbag flats.'

'I know. What's the game, Quinn?'

'I'm offering twenty grand for the kid.'

'I think Mr Buck here would put it down your throat with his fist.'

'Buck? Who's he?'

'He's with Shelley.'

'Sounds like a nigger.'

'He's a Maori.'

'Shit! I'm gonna have to keep real close tabs on Shelley now you've found her for me and I don't think she's gonna like it. I'm gettin' that kid, Hardy, if it takes me a year. I never had a kid.'

'That's a blessing. Why'd you use me? Why not one of your men, as you call them?'

'They've got no finesse. I wanted it to look genuine. You did a great job, Hardy. Thanks.'

I hung up on him which felt good but didn't help. Buck changed Tommy's nappy and Shelley put him down for a sleep. We drank more coffee while the little flat got hotter. After my anger at being used by Quinn had receded I began thinking again.

'We have to get something on him,' I said. 'Shelley, can you remember anything he was sensitive about. D'you know anything about his business dealings?'

She shook her head. 'No, nothing. Sensitive? Him? You're kidding. All that Norman Mailer crap, the photograph ... Hold on, there *was* something. He got angry when I looked at this old picture I found.'

'What picture?'

'It was real old. It looked like a newspaper picture but it was, you know, glossy. It was a boxing picture. Two guys in the ring and a lot of people crowding around. I know Henry was a boxer.'

'Was he in the picture?'

'Hard to say. It was old. If it was him he had a lot more hair and no gut. I don't know. Anyway, he hit me.'

'Jesus.' Peter Buck cracked his knuckles.

'Can you remember anything else about the picture?'

'Nuh. Yes, there was a woman in it. A blonde. She was yelling. That's all.'

I felt a twinge of hope. 'How're you for money?'

'Low,' Buck said.

I put three hundred dollars on the table and took out one of my cards. 'I might have a way. What you have to do is get together a few blokes to keep an eye on Shelley and Tommy. Round the clock. Can you do it?'

'Sure.'

'Don't look for trouble. Just make sure those characters outside never get close. Ring me if you have a problem.'

'Why're you doing this?' Shelley said.

'I don't like feeling dumb. I'm sorry about your knee.'

Buck grinned. 'You'll have me in tears. Work something out pretty quick or I'll handle it my way.'

I waited at the flat until two men arrived—another Maori and a pakeha, both tattooed, both big. The Maori was carrying a big bottle of lemonade, a bucket of fried chicken and a towel. He flicked the towel at Buck. 'Let's go to the beach.'

'That's the spirit,' I said.

I took a look at the men in the green car before I got into the Falcon—average-looking thugs, not very bright. They stayed put and I drove to the Public Library. The public records are hell when you don't know what you're looking for, heaven when you do. It didn't take me long; on November 29, 1956, the Melbourne *Sun News-Pictorial* had published an Olympic Games photograph in its sports section. The picture showed the scene after US light heavyweight Hank Quinn had been disqualified for eye gouging in his bout with Australian Ian Madison. A younger, fitter Quinn stood defiant in centre ring while Madison held both gloves across his face. A blonde woman shrieked at the referee from ringside. The brief account of the fight was highly critical of Quinn and mentioned that his wife, Billie, had attempted to assault the referee after the disqualification was announced. I took a copy of the microfilm frames.

It was four o'clock when I got home to Glebe. I was hungry and thirsty but optimistic. I drank two glasses of wine and ate a slice of fairly old pizza. Then I phoned my lawyer, Cy Sackville.

'You're lucky to catch me,' Cy said. 'I'm going to Byron Bay for Christmas.'

'Good on you. Would you have a contact in New York who'd be able to look up marriage records in New Jersey and locate a certain party?'

'Of course.'

'And you'd have a fax machine there in the office, wouldn't you?'

'Of course.'

'What about US Treasury records, tax assessments and so on?'

'Harder but possible. You thinking of moving

offshore, Cliff? Thought you were more patriotic than that.'

I laughed dutifully and told him what I wanted. He said 'Um' and 'Yes' and told me there'd be someone in his office to handle whatever came in.

'What'll it cost?' I asked.

'It's Christmas.'

After that it was a matter of waiting. I went out to Manly the next couple of days and we had some fun on the beach—Shelley, Peter Buck, Tommy, Eddie Tongarira and a Manly reserve grade front rower named Steve. The men up under the pines who watched us looked hot and bothered.

The information from the States came through on Christmas Eve; first I phoned Shelley, then Quinn.

'Quinn? This is Hardy. We'd like to come to the party tomorrow. Is it still on?'

'Who's we?' Quinn sounded suspicious and a bit drunk.

'Shelley, Peter Buck, me and Tommy. You should have the thousand you owe me ready.'

His laugh was a raucous, tipsy bellow. 'That right? You seein' sense? You're not such a . . . what is it? Not such a mug as I took you for. Make it early. Ten o'clock. You say the kid'll be along? I'll get a tree.'

I got to the Manly flat a bit before eight. The green car was outside. Everybody had been awake for three hours and the place was a sea of wrapping paper and cardboard boxes. I had a can with Peter and Shelley and the minders and then we set off for Cronulla with the green car following. One of the watchers joined us in the lift and he and Peter Buck eyed each other off as we rode up to Quinn's penthouse.

Quinn was wearing a pink shirt and white trousers. He'd shaved extra close and done something to his hair. He looked even more like the photograph of Mailer than before.

'Shelley,' he boomed. 'So good to see ya, honey. An' this must be the boy. How ya doin', sonny?' He attempted to kiss Tommy's cheek but Tommy belched.

'Cute,' Quinn said. 'C'mon in. You can go, Lenny.' The watcher withdrew and we went into the room that seemed to be half-filled with sun and sea and sky. Pine needles from a huge Christmas tree by the window lay all over the carpet. At least ten wrapped presents were piled up under the tree. Shelley, Peter Buck and Tommy sat on the leather couch. Quinn pulled a bottle of champagne from an ice bucket and clawed off the foil wrapping. His hands were shaking.

'Let's have a drink.'

'Let's see the money,' I said.

'Oh, sure, sure. He reached into his hip pocket and pulled out a wad of notes. 'Two grand. Bonus. You can't say Henry Quinn's cheap.'

I took the money and handed it to Shelley. Neither she nor Buck had said a word. Tommy was sleeping in Peter's arms.

'What is this?' Quinn said.

I took the bottle from him, popped the cork and poured the champagne into four long glasses. I pushed Quinn down into a chair, gave him a glass and carried two to the couch. I took a sip of mine and reached into my pocket. Quinn clutched his glass and stared at me. I spread out the documents on the arm of his chair.

'This is a photograph of you losing in Melbourne in '56. Your wife Billie isn't happy but you lost just the same. This is a photostat of your marriage certificate. Henry Quinn bachelor, blah, blah, Billie Teresa D'Angelo, spinster, blah, blah, Atlantic

City, New Jersey, May 8, 1955. No divorce ever registered. Billie Quinn, welfare recipient, Century Hotel, Atlantic City, deposes December 23, 1986, that no divorce ever took place on account of both parties were of the Catholic faith. Here is a US Treasury memo to the effect that Henry Xavier Quinn is liable for US taxes of more than one million dollars but, ah, I'm quoting, "action is forestalled due to Quinn's status as an Australian resident alien".' I looked across at the couch. Shelley and Peter Buck touched glasses and drank.

'Shit,' Quinn said.

I sipped some of the champagne. 'Your status here depends on your marriage to Dawn Leonie Simkin in 1958, but that marriage was bigamous which means that you ain't got no status at all.'

Quinn twitched and spilled champagne; a dark stain appeared on his pink shirt. 'You bastard,' he said.

'How'd you like to be deported, Henry? How'd you like to get into a plea bargaining situation with the US Treasury? I think you'd rather stay here, wouldn't you? I think you'd rather stay childless but well-heeled and very, very quiet, eh?'

'Yes,' Quinn said.

'Okay. You've got a deal.'

Shelley and Peter finished their champagne and stood up. Buck hoisted Tommy on to his shoulder and put his glass down carefully on a polished table, 'Thanks, Hardy. Come on, Shell.'

'Call the next one Cliff,' I said. 'Hang on, I'm coming with you'. I tapped the documents together and put them in Quinn's lap. The wetness had spread down over his paunch. 'These are copies.' I reached out and patted his smooth-shaved cheek. 'Merry Christmas, Norman,' I said.

In slightly different versions, 'Cloudburst', 'The Deserter' and 'High Integrity' have appeared in Australian *Penthouse*. Minus its present ending, 'Byron Kelly's Big Mistake' was published in the *Sydney Morning Herald* weekly magazine *Good Weekend*. 'Norman Mailer's Christmas' was published in the *Sydney Morning Herald*.